Someone—or something—had stopped Marta from telling her story. Would they silence Ina, too?

In an isolated chalet in the Austrian Alps, Ina learns that the evils of the past often return to haunt in the present. Satan is waiting on the slopes . . .

OTHER WARNER PAPERBACK LIBRARY BOOKS
BY MARILYN ROSS

Step Into Terror
The Devil's Daughter
The Sinister Garden
Night of the Phantom
Mistress of Moorwood Manor
The Witch of Bralhaven
The Long Night of Fear
Phantom of the Swamp
Dark Stars Over Seacrest
Message From a Ghost
Phantom of Fog Island

Witches' Cove
The Aquarius Curse
Shorecliff
Satan's Rock
Phantom Manor
Mistress of Ravenswood
Memory of Evil
A Gathering of Evil
Desperate Heiress
Beware My Love

THE DARK SHADOWS SERIES

Barnabas, Quentin and the Vampire Beauty
Barnabas, Quentin and the Hidden Tomb
Barnabas, Quentin and the Mad Magician
Barnabas, Quentin and the Sea Ghost
Barnabas, Quentin and the Grave Robbers
Barnabas, Quentin and Dr. Jekyll's Son
Barnabas, Quentin and the Body Snatchers
Barnabas, Quentin and the Magic Potion
Barnabas, Quentin and the Serpent
Barnabas, Quentin and the Scorpio Curse
Barnabas, Quentin and the Frightened Bride
Barnabas, Quentin and the Haunted Cave
Barnabas, Quentin and the Witch's Curse
Barnabas, Quentin and the Crystal Coffin
Barnabas, Quentin and the Nightmare Assassin
Barnabas, Quentin and the Avenging Ghost
Barnabas, Quentin and the Mummy's Curse
Barnabas Collins and the Gypsy Witch
Barnabas Collins and Quentin's Demon
Barnabas Collins and the Mysterious Ghost
The Peril of Barnabas Collins
Barnabas Collins Versus the Warlock
The Phantom and Barnabas Collins
The Foe of Barnabas Collins
The Secret of Barnabas Collins
The Demon of Barnabas Collins
The Curse of Collinwood
Strangers at Collins House
The Mystery of Collinwood
Victoria Winters
Dark Shadows
Barnabas Collins

Marta
Marilyn Ross

WARNER
PAPERBACK LIBRARY
NEW YORK

WARNER PAPERBACK LIBRARY EDITION
First Printing: March, 1973

Copyright © 1973 by Marilyn Ross
All rights reserved

Cover illustration by Franco Accornero

Warner Paperback Library is a division of Warner Books, Inc., 315 Park Avenue South, New York, N.Y. 10010.

MARTA

CHAPTER ONE

It began with the arrival at the East Sixty-Fourth Street apartment in New York City where Ina Sperling lived with her widowed mother of an airmail letter with an Austrian postmark. And it proved to be the beginning of a series of weird events which culminated in the rollicking yet somewhat eerie atmosphere of a costume ball held in a great, gothic castle in honor of the *Faschingsdienstag,* the Alpine Mardi Gras.

Though Ina Sperling had no knowledge of it then, the letter was to take her to the Tyrolean ski center of St. Anton and involve her in a strange adventure whose beginnings went back to Nazi Germany and centered around a glamorous young screen actress of that now distant era. Ghosts from the past would intrude themselves in her life and her very existence would be threatened by ghostly hands reaching out from the troubled past!

She would live in an isolated chalet in the shadow of great snow-capped mountains, overlooking the picturesque village of St. Anton, its buildings showing twinkling lights in the cold darkness as they huddled together in the snow of the valley below. And she would meet the gay international set gathered for skiing and the exciting après-ski parties as well as the ordinary people, the women in their native full dirndl skirts and lace blouses and the men in gray wool suits and leather pants.

She would discover the strong Germanic strain of these

Tyrol folk and remember that Hitler had chosen Austria as the site for Berchtesgaden, his mountain retreat. And she would hear some of the ghostly legends which had their origin in the Hitler era; tales told of the haunted voices of long-dead Hitler youths who sang sad German songs as they gathered around phantom campfires on dark, stormy nights, their ghostly voices echoing a lament to a twisted dream which had died with them.

She was also to be awed by the story of a very special kind of ghost—the ghost of Karl Bruck! The name of Karl Bruck was largely forgotten now except in that section of the Austrian alps and in the various histories of Germany before and during the Second World War. For Bruck had been a high-ranking and trusted aide to Adolph Hitler during those turbulent years who had owned a fine chalet on the mountainside above St. Anton. He had been a familiar figure on the ski slopes there during the days when he was in power.

The natives still remembered him, though he must have been ordinary enough in appearance from their accounts. A mild-looking, round-faced man, he only showed his cruel, steel character in hard blue eyes, in one of which he wore a monocle. The monocle was his only affectation. He skiied well and now beside the blazing inn fireplaces were told stories of his phantom figure coursing down the highest ski slopes in the moonlight! For Karl Bruck had been one of those who a quarter of a century ago had died beside Hitler in that Berlin bunker.

But all this was to come later. At the moment when the letter had arrived she'd been in the study of the apartment working on a magazine article. At twenty-five, Ina was a well-known freelance journalist and the author of two best-selling biographies, one of a celebrated pianist and the other of a rather shady politician. Her competitors scornfully pointed out that her clear-skinned, even beauty and flowing tawny hair had a lot to do with her popularity with editors. But most of the literary critics felt she had unusual talent.

Her mother took care of phone calls and other details

while Ina was writing. And only when she emerged from her study for a noon break did she get a chance to quickly run over the morning's mail. On this December midday when she left her work to join her mother in the well-furnished living room of their pleasant apartment, she discovered her mother in a state of great excitement.

As Ina approached the desk with the stack of mail on it, Helen Sperling came to join her and with her eyes wide, asked her, "Who do you think you have a letter from today?"

"I'm not good at guessing games," she reminded her mother.

Helen pointed to the colored airmail envelope on the top of the pile of mail where she'd placed it. "You have a letter from Austria! From Marta Landen!"

Ina's intelligent oval face registered surprise. "From Marta Landen!"

"That's right," her mother said triumphantly, satisfied that she'd been able to surprise her.

Ina picked up the unopened envelope in a slim hand and stared at it in amazement. "It's probably a Christmas card. That's what we've mostly had in the mail lately."

"I don't think so," her mother said. "It doesn't look like a Christmas card, and anyway Marta has never bothered to send us any in the past. Why should she suddenly begin now?"

"I have no idea," Ina admitted. "We may as well see what it is all about." And she opened the letter and began reading it.

After a moment her mother asked. "What does it say?"

Ina glanced up from the letter. "It's rather strange and not too clear."

"Read it to me," her mother urged her.

"Very well," she said, and began: "My dear Ina, it has been too long since I've been in touch with you. But the years have gone by so swiftly. I remember our one meeting in Hollywood about fifteen years ago when you and your mother came to visit me there. I was under so much studio tension at the time, I did not find myself in the mood to entertain you properly. But I have remembered you.

"When I married your father's brother so many years ago, you were only a baby. It is hard to imagine you all grown up and a name in the writing world! You will see that I have followed your career with great interest. The death of your Uncle Ralph so soon after our marriage was a crisis in my life and brought me great sadness. And that he had his drowning accident in a stream so near our chalet made it doubly tragic. Had he not been alone when he suffered his heart seizure, he might have been saved.

"I'm grateful that he lived long enough to give me a daughter, and your cousin, Gretchen, has grown into a beauty. Unfortunately she is interested in an acting career but lacks my talent and so has developed certain feelings of frustration. However, we do have a good life here in our mountain retreat.

"My present husband David Leopold is a dear man and devotes a great deal of his time to gathering mementos of my career and keeping my name before the world press. I fear I am not as much in demand as I once was. But I have made several very fine pictures in London and Rome during the past year, though I've only played supporting parts.

"Our adopted son, Claude, is pursuing his career as a concert violinist and rapidly becoming a name in the field. He is coming home for a visit in January.

"I trust your good mother is in her usual excellent health. I ask that you give her my warmest regards. And now I shall explain the real purpose of my letter. I have come to the time of life when I feel I would like to set down all the facts. As you know, I have had a fairly full and exciting career both in Europe and America. I think the publication of an authentic biography at this time might spark my professional life again, remind people of me and get me some new job offers. Not that I need the money, far from it, but I do want the excitement and challenge of working.

"My husband, David, is not enthusiastic about the project, but I am. I tried to start with it about two years ago, but the young man I engaged to ghost write the book for me proved unequal to the task. So I'm left with it still unfinished.

"I feel you are the one to do it. You know me fairly well and I have confidence in you. I do share family bonds with you through marriage. I'm willing to let you have the full proceeds of any sale of the work and I urge you to visit me at my chalet here in St. Anton.

"It is high season here and will be so for weeks to come. If you see fit to be my guest, you will have the opportunity of meeting David and my adopted son, Claude, and perhaps we may be able to arrive at some working agreement about the book. Cable me if the idea appeals to you, and you could join us directly after the New Year holiday. When I hear from you I shall rush instructions as to how best to find us. I hope you will see fit to come. All good holiday wishes to you and your mother. Sincerely, Marta."

Ina put the letter down. "What do you make of it?"

Her mother was a plain woman who had lately been wearing dark pant suits during the daytime. She was wearing a dark brown one now as she slumped into a nearby easy chair and stared up at Ina in astonishment.

"The letter is surely long enough!"

"I know."

"And she's still as arrogant and unthinking of others as ever," her mother exclaimed. "Still the great star expecting everyone to bow and scrape to her."

Ina smiled thinly. "I don't think there is any arrogance in her letter."

"I say you're wrong," Helen Sperling said. "She's asking you to drop everything here and hurry half across the world to discuss her problems. I call that unthinking of her!"

"It happens that I will be free of assignments in January," Ina said.

"She couldn't know that. And I'm sure she'd be impossible to work with anyway. You remember what she was like in Hollywood! The very model of a temperamental foreign star!"

"I don't recall it too well," Ina admitted. "I was only ten at the time of our visit. She's fifteen years older now, perhaps she has mellowed."

"I very much doubt that," her mother said. "People like Marta don't change. She was Germany's most popular feminine star in her teens. Everyone spoiled her."

"Uncle Ralph must have found her attractive," Ina pointed out, "or he wouldn't have married her."

"She's attractive enough but there's a cruel, demanding side of her. Your Uncle Ralph was a playwright. He knew how to cope with show-business people. I've never been fond of them. Nor was your father. And I'm sure we all agreed that your Uncle Ralph might still be alive if he hadn't married Marta and gone over there to live with that fast crowd. There was a good deal of mystery about his drowning, you know."

Ina lifted her shapely eyebrows. "Mystery?"

Her mother nodded. "He'd had no record of heart weakness and yet he had a fatal seizure while swimming in a stream near their chalet. He was alone at the time and was dead when they found him. Your father always felt that Ralph had been drinking."

"You can't blame that on Marta. She writes as if she had been very fond of him."

"She would now," her mother said bitterly. "But I can't recall that she showed much grief at the time. Your Uncle Ralph's ashes were shipped back here and she didn't come with them. After that your father refused to have anything to do with Marta. And it was only after his death that we made our visit to Hollywood to see her. And it was hardly a success."

Ina sighed. "Still, we must be fair to her. She was probably working at the time of Uncle Ralph's death and so it would have been hard for her to come here with his remains. And she seems friendly enough and anxious to give me a chance to do her story. Certainly her terms are generous."

Her mother's lips were set in a grim line. "I still say I don't trust her or her motives."

Ina saw that the discussion was leading nowhere. Her mother had decided views about the famous screen star and nothing was going to change them. She told her mother, "You get lunch ready and I'll skim through the rest of this mail. And we can talk more about Marta over lunch."

She sat at the desk and went quickly over bills, notices, Christmas cards, and found a letter from an editor suggesting a new project for her to begin after the New Year. It struck her as a coincidence that she should receive two offers in the same mail. She put this letter away in a private file folder for the moment and decided not to tell her mother anything about it.

By this time her mother was calling her to join her at a coffee table in the living rom where she'd put out on a tray some sandwiches and coffee. Ina sat on the divan facing the table and helped herself to a sandwich.

Glancing at her mother in an easy chair opposite her, she said, "I know you're going to be upset. But I find Marta Landen's offer too good to resist. I'm going to cable her I'll join her after the New Year."

Helen Sperling shook her head. "I was afraid you were going to say something like that!"

"I think it's a great opportunity!" Ina exclaimed. "Marta has had a long and colorful career. It could make a best-selling book. And I need a good theme right now."

Her mother frowned. "I'll worry about you every minute you are over there."

"Ridiculous!" she protested, laughing. "I'm a grown girl now. And I'll have a chance to work in some skiing as well as discussing the book with Marta."

"You know what she was!" her mother warned her with a look of disapproval.

Ina stared at her. "Now what are you saying?"

"I'm simply telling you that a lot of Marta's past is more sordid than colorful," her mother said urgently. "It was in all the papers when she came here after the war to star in a Broadway play. Your Uncle Ralph defended her but he made a mistake. For a while there was a question of whether she'd be allowed to remain in this country."

Ina listened with amazement. "You mean because it was so soon after the war and she was German? Why should that matter? I think she was being unfairly treated!"

"The press claimed that not only was she a German but she had also been a Nazi," Helen Sperling said tautly. "And from what your father and Uncle Ralph said when they talked about it here one night, the papers were right. Of course your Uncle Ralph felt she'd only been a young girl at the time and should be forgiven. He used all his influence to get some favorable news items about her, and she was forgiven. She stayed and played the show and then married Ralph."

"So she couldn't have been all that bad," Ina said.

"I don't know about that," her mother replied. "She was surely a favorite of Hitler's circle and her name was directly linked with the notorious Karl Bruck, one of Hitler's most hated SS men. He built her the chalet in which she lives in St. Anton now, if rumor is correct. Of course she claims it was the other way around, that she had always owned the chalet and Bruck was merely her guest a few times."

"That could be true."

Helen Sperling looked grim. "I doubt it. Anyway, she managed to make people believe the story and she still lives there. She remained there during the collapse of Germany when Karl Bruck died in that Berlin bunker with Hitler. Then she went to England and starred in a film and following that came here to play on Broadway and meet your uncle."

"She has a daughter my age," Ina reminded her mother. "Gretchen! I think I should meet my cousin!"

"From the letter it sounds as if she might be a lot like Marta. Marta didn't take her to Hollywood with her, so we didn't meet her on that visit we made there."

"Gretchen should be company for me, and she'll be able to introduce me to friends of our own age."

"Perhaps I'm prejudiced," her mother admitted. "But I still am of the opinion that Marta Landen is a product of the Nazi days of her girlhood. I'm sure she must have been associated with all kinds of dreadful people and likely a party to many wicked plots. Some of those people must still be alive and lurking in the background. I can't imagine them relishing the idea of her telling all in a book to bring her back in the limelight. There could be danger in such an undertaking for both you and her!"

Ina laughed as she poured herself some coffee. "Now you sound silly! The war has been over for twenty-five years! Most of the people who had an active part in things then are dead or very old."

"Marta is only fifty-four or five."

"She's an exception. She was a young girl when all that took place. I can't see that she could have been in on any deep secrets. She may have known these people and been a plaything for them, but I doubt if she was anything more. She may have even known Hitler! Think how exciting it would be if she had some new stories to tell about him!"

Her mother looked upset. "I have never found anything inspiring about Hitler or his associates, and I've made it a point to avoid reading about them!"

"But you're not the average reader, Mother," Ina protested. "People like sensationalism, and books on the Hitler era still sell."

"Marta won't want to talk much about that part of her life if I know her," Helen Sperling said. "She's done all possible to make people forget. After your Uncle Ralph's drowning she married a nice man she'd befriended, a former businessman who has looked after her affairs since, a Jewish man named David Leopold. I'm sure the fact he was a Jew made her anxious to marry him. It helped clean away her past."

Ina said, "She mentioned him in the letter. And I'm sure you are being very unfair. You say she and this David were friends before Uncle Ralph's death. Undoubtedly she was in love with him and the fact he was Jewish was no more than coincidence."

"They adopted a Jewish boy, a survivor of the concentration camps like David Leopold. That's the Claude she mentions who has become a famous violinist. Again I'm positive she did that to try and brighten her reputation and make people forget she'd been a Nazi darling."

"To marry a Jewish man and then adopt a boy of the same religion who had suffered seems natural and commendable to me," Ina said. "Even if she adopted the boy because she felt some guilt, it was a good thing to do. I'm sure she has repented for any of her early associations."

Her mother sighed. "I can see you want to believe that."

"I do. This woman is related to us by marriage. Her daughter is my blood cousin! I can't picture them as villains!"

"Your father was never happy about the marriage."

"I still feel that I should go to Austria and meet them," Ina said. "And I will. And when I return with a good book, you'll be the first to congratulate me."

Her mother gave her a worried look. "Naturally I hope it turns out well. But I don't like the idea at all. And I hope you change your mind."

Ina didn't change her mind. She promptly sent a cable to her Aunt Marta and said she would like to join her right after the New Year. A cable came back immediately with the terse message: DELIGHTED. TAKE PLANE TO PARIS AND EXPRESS TRAIN TO ZURICH AND VIENNA WHICH STOPS AT ST. ANTON. FONDLY, MARTA.

Ina deferred all her other projects and made plans to leave New York for Paris two days after the New Year. She arranged through a travel agent to make a connecting booking on the Alberg express which would take her directly to St. Anton. Fortunately, her mother was kept so busy with holiday preparations that she hadn't any time to argue with her about the proposed trip.

In the meantime Ina made it her business to do some

research on Marta Landen. There was quite a lot of material in the New York Public Library and she discovered that much of what her mother had told her was true. Ina pored over the ancient news clippings and photographs of the smiling dark-haired beauty and gradually came to realize that she must have surely been very close to the Nazi rulers of Germany in that day.

One photograph showed her standing by Karl Bruck as he took a Nazi salute from a group of dedicated youths. But the photo was so blurred, it was hard for her to really study the faces of the two. It would be difficult to tell whether Marta's expression was approving or not. And since she was only about nineteen at the time the photo had been taken, it seemed to Ina that the girl shouldn't have been censured too severely for her choice of companions. She had been very young, and rising to stardom could not have been easy without being friendly to certain important people.

Karl Bruck surely had been one of those people. And by Ina's figuring, he must have been in his late thirties at the time he'd become interested in the nineteen-year-old Marta. According to the news item, he had been in his early forties when his body had been found in the bunker with the burned bodies of Hitler and his mistress.

It was while she was doing her research on Marta in America that she came on the name of the Broadway producer who had starred in a play at the Empire Theatre. She knew that the theatre had long been razed to make way for an office building, but the name of the producer, Pat Brody, was occasionally mentioned in *The New York Times* Sunday theatre section. She decided to contact the drama editor at the *Times* and find out if Brody might be reached.

She discovered that Brody was a semi-invalid and living in a shabby though respectable hotel not far from Lincoln Center which was a favorite with fringe theatre people and forgotten names of other years. She put a call through to him and he answered the phone himself in the wheezed voice of a chronic asthma sufferer.

"Do you remember Marta Landen?" she queried him.

"Yes," the old man at the other end of the line wheezed. "Why?"

"I may be doing a book on her," she said. "I'm Ralph Sperling's niece. You must remember him. The playwright."

"Sure, I knew Ralph," the old man said, then coughing for a moment. After he'd cleared his throat, he said, "I did one of Ralph's plays. He married Marta, didn't he?"

"Yes. But he's been dead a long while."

"I remember."

She said, "Would it be possible for me to call on you? I'd like to ask you some questions."

The old man seemed pleased that she should have an interest in him. "Any time," he said, with a cough. "I haven't been too well. I never leave my room."

So she made an appointment for the next afternoon. She spent a little time braving the Christmas shopping crowd to get a present for her mother. Then she took the subway uptown. When she got out at Lincoln Center, it was snowing. But it wasn't laying down a clean surface. It was a soft, wet snow and settled down murkily, turning quickly into slush. Truly miserable weather, Ina thought.

She reached the stately old hotel which showed many signs of neglect in spite of its fine architecture. All the ground floor had been taken over by small, shabby stores with red neon signs. The entrance to the hotel had been cut down to make room for these, and the lobby was dark and smelled of stale tobacco smoke. She approached the desk where a thin, bald-headed man waited.

She said, "I'd like to see Mr. Pat Brody."

He eyed her suspiciously. "Does he know you're coming?"

Her cheeks burned under his hard scrutiny. She decided he was probably used to girls attempting to reach the upper regions of the hotel on one excuse or another. She said, "Yes. My name is Sperling. Ina Sperling. I have an appointment to interview him."

"Yeah?" The bald man continued to look and sound

doubtful. He moved to the switchboard, still keeping a close eye on her, and called Pat Brody's room. "Girl here claims she has an appointment with you." There was a pause and then he said, "Okay," with a look of disappointment on his white, beard-stubbled face. He gave Ina a glance of annoyance. "Room 924," he snapped.

"Thank you," she said, anxious to be on her way, and made for the nearest of the two self-service elevators.

As she reached it, two husky youths speaking excitedly in Spanish got off. One of them smiled and gave her the eye before they moved on out toward the lobby. Hastily she got in the elevator and pressed the button for the ninth floor. After an interminable time the elevator started up slowly with an alarming background sound of straining. The ninth floor came with a jolt and she stepped out into the dark hallway.

It took her a moment to adjust to the dim light of the corridor. Then she studied the nearest doors for numbers and discovered that 924 was down to the right. She made her way down the dark, smelly corridor with considerable misgivings. It seemed that she might have made a mistake coming to such a place.

At last she reached 924 and knocked on the door. After a moment she heard someone coughing inside and then shuffling footsteps approaching the door. There was the sound of a key turning in a lock and then a bolt being slid back. Next the door opened a small crack and someone peered out at her.

She said, "I'm Ina Sperling."

"Miss Sperling!" came the delighted response from the other side of the door chain in a wheezed voice. And he unhooked the chain to open the door wide.

Ina stepped into the room. It was much brighter than the hall, though just as shabby. Pat Brody shut the door and bolted it again. He was a stout old man with a mane of white hair and a ruddy, double-chinned face. His eyes were gray and still remarkably young, though he seemed old and infirm in every other way.

He led her into the room, racked by a spell of coughing

once again. It was a bed-sitting room; the daybed was open and unmade, with rumpled bedclothes on it.

"You'll have to overlook the appearance of this place," he apologized. "I spend most of my time in bed."

"I'm sorry to bother you," she said.

"Glad you did," Brody wheezed. "Everyone seems to think I'm dead. There are days when I'm even ready to believe it. Good to have somebody from the outside world contact me."

"You knew my Uncle Ralph," she said.

The white head nodded. "I can see a little of him in you. Sit down." He coughed again and held a soiled white handkerchief over his mouth. He was dressed in a red silk robe which must have dated back to more prosperous days. Under it he had on heavy blue flannel pajamas, with worn slippers on his feet.

She sat in a plain chair with a cane seat and back while he slumped down on the side of his bed, clearing his throat and seeming to find it difficult to breathe.

She said, "If you're not feeling well, I can come back again."

He raised a hand to protest. "No. I'm fine. Better than I am most days. It's my heart condition complicated by this asthma that has made me a shut-in."

"I'm sorry," she said.

He sighed. "Hadn't many places to go anyway. Used to drop by the Lambs Club. Some of them come up here to call on me every so often. Not the young, active members; they're too busy. It's the old fellows retired from the game like myself who show up. But I hardly ever see a face as young and pretty as yours."

"Thank you," she said. "So you really did have Marta Landen in a play?"

He nodded. "I made a pile of money on that show. She was in the news a lot and the publicity paid off. I guess you wonder what I'm doing in a hotel like this if I made so much money. Well, I'll tell you. All my productions weren't that successful. I lost plenty before I had to give up."

"I'm sure producing plays is a risky business."

"Gamble," he coughed. "Purely a gamble."

"About Marta Landen. Did you like her?"

Pat Brody's broad ruddy face showed surprise. "Did I like her? I don't know. Never thought about that. But I didn't trust her."

"Oh? Why not?"

His stout old body shook with coughing again and it was a moment before he managed to stop and clear his throat. "You must know a lot about her now," he said. "You've been digging for stuff."

"I have," she said. "But I'd like a real opinion of what she was like from the lips of someone who knew her at that time. You're probably the only one."

He coughed and held his fist to his lips for a minute. Then he lowered it and said, "Lone survivor! That's me, all right. What was Marta like? She was beautiful and she was dangerous."

Ina looked up from the small book in which she'd been taking down his words. "Now you fascinate me. How do you mean dangerous?"

The young eyes sparkled as they fixed on her. "Just what I say. Marta was used to playing a lone game. She'd do anything just so long as she could see it would help her. She didn't care about anyone else. She was used to taking care of Marta and that was that!"

"My mother remembers her as arrogant. What do you say?"

"She was that all right. And sharp. She had her agent set up a hard deal with me. But she gave a great performance. She was worth the trouble."

"What do you feel about her relationship with the Nazis?"

Brody shrugged. "You can't deny it."

"Do you think she was one of them? She was very young at the time."

A grim smile spread across the old man's ruddy face. "I don't think you can excuse her on that." He coughed. "She was the sort who grew up fast. I think she played along with the Hitler crowd while it helped her. When they were done, so was she. Marta thinks of Marta first!"

"I'm planning to go visit her," Ina said. "She wants me to help her write the story of her life."

The old producer was bracing himself on the bed with his two hands firmly planted on the mattress on either side of him. He gave a deep sigh. "Should be some story."

"I think so," she said. "I hope so. I'm interested in hearing about those early days in Germany. It's something the public will buy."

Pat Brody cleared his throat. It had become as ordinary to him as breathing. He said, "Did she tell you she'd talk?"

"She hinted it."

"I'd be careful if I were you," the old man said, surprising her with his caution. "There could be a few people around still who wouldn't want her telling things about them."

Ina was shocked. "You think that? After this long while."

He nodded grimly. "She was in deep."

Ina hesitated. The interview wasn't too satisfactory. It was turning out too much like her talks with her mother. She felt the old man had not been able to contribute much.

She said, "That was long ago. People have forgotten."

"Don't be too sure," Pat Brody warned her. "I suppose that is why Marta is anxious to tell her story now, before everyone does forget. She probably counts on it putting her in the limelight again."

"I think so. She hasn't had too many screen roles lately."

He coughed. "Then she'll talk plenty. And she should have a lot to tell you. Give her my regards."

"I will."

"But don't tell her what an old wreck I've become," he begged her.

"I wouldn't think of it," she said, smiling as she closed her notebook, feeling that the interview had come to an end.

"Marta had a child by your uncle, didn't she?"

"Yes. A girl. We've never met."

"Your cousin! That should be interesting," the old man wheezed. "Especially since she's part Marta."

"I understand she's also been trying a screen career."

A cunning smile crossed Brody's face. "I'll bet that Marta hasn't tried to help her. She wouldn't want another star in the family. Not Marta!"

Ina was surprised. "I don't know. She just mentioned it in a letter to me. She hinted the girl hadn't been too successful."

Pat Brody chuckled. "See if I'm not right."

"I will," she said, rising.

The old man still sat on the side of the day bed. "You've made up your mind to go over there?"

"Yes."

"She's still living in Bruck's chalet?"

"I understand it was always hers. She's married again. To a man who came out of the concentration camps. And she also adopted a Jewish boy. He's grown-up now."

Pat Brody nodded. "Marta always did the smart thing. And you can bet she has some angle in mind in writing this book on her life. She's a keen operator."

Ina felt it was time to leave. She said, "Thanks for giving me this time."

He waved a pudgy hand. "I have all the time in the world. That's my problem these days."

She smiled sympathetically. "I hope you're better soon."

"Don't count on it," he said, striving for breath and then clearing his throat again.

"I'll let you know about the book," she said, taking a step toward the door. "If I write it, you'll likely be in it."

"I'd like that," the old man said.

"I'll certainly devote a section to her experiences on the New York stage," Ina said. "And of course I'll tell of her romance with Uncle Ralph."

Pat Brody said, "I often wondered why he married her. Only conclusion I could come to was that she hypnotized him with her talent and beauty."

She raised her brows. "Weren't they in love?"

"I suppose so," the old man said. "But Ralph left a lot behind him when he went back to Austria with her. I know they planned to come back here and do other plays and movies. But he never lived to see that happen."

"He did die suddenly."

The old man coughed and then stared at her with those oddly youthful eyes. "That's another thing that bothered me. Ralph had always had good health."

"Heart attacks do strike without warning."

"I suppose so," Brody said. "But I think Ralph had a sort of premonition about his death."

She stared at the producer. "Why do you say that?"

"I had a letter or two from him. He was discussing the production of a new play he was working on for me. It was about the Hitler crowd, and we both thought it would make a hit. Marta had given him plenty of inside stuff. And he wrote me, If I live to finish this one, I think I'll strike the jackpot."

She said, "You couldn't call that odd. People often say such things without meaning anything at all."

"I suppose so," the old man agreed. "But I've thought about it since. Ralph was dead a few weeks later."

"What about the play?"

He gave her a strange look. "I never saw it. I wrote Marta after his death and she claimed she couldn't find it. She said he must have gotten dissatisfied with it and destroyed it. But I couldn't buy that. Not when I knew how enthusiastic he'd been about the play."

She stood there in the growing darkness of the room with an eerie feeling suddenly surging through her. "What do you think happened to it?"

Pat Brody sighed. "I think for one reason or another Marta destroyed the manuscript."

CHAPTER TWO

All the way back downtown in the subway, the old man's words haunted her. Marta must have destroyed the play her Uncle Ralph had written, with its revelations about the high-ranking Nazis. Could that be the answer to his sudden death? Had his drowning somehow been manipulated so that the play would never be produced?

All that had happened long ago when the war was only shortly ended. There could have been members of the party still anxious to protect themselves against exposure. They might have engineered her uncle's death. But if so, wouldn't Marta have known? According to the elderly theatrical producer, it could be entirely possible that Marta had known and let it happen, as it involved her own safety.

These thoughts were alarming, so much so that she refused to credit them. She was sure that Pat Brody had made more of the situation than was called for and that her mother was also unduly prejudiced against Marta Landen. It was in a way an example of the generation gap. These two older people were part of the war generation and so still held suspicious fears of the long-vanished Nazis. She knew no such fear.

She had learned little from her chat with Pat Brody, but it had been an interesting experience. Likely she would see him again on her return from Austria. She would want to discuss the play Marta had starred in at great length with him then. It would be part of her book.

Already she was excited about going to Austria. She had been in Vienna briefly when she'd taken a short tour of Europe. But she had not had time to visit the Austrian countryside or see the Tyrolean Alps. She had been there in summer, but now she would be arriving at the height of the winter sports season. And in St. Anton winter sports meant skiing.

Christmas and New Year's went by and she was ready to leave for Europe. Her mother became tearful as it came time for her to take a taxi to Kennedy Airport.

Helen Sperling sobbed, "I do wish you'd change your mind. It's still not too late to cancel out."

"I have to go," Ina protested. "Everything is booked, the taxi is waiting and Marta is expecting me."

"You should have given this more thought," her mother worried. "I'll be on edge all the time you're gone."

"I'll send you a cable as soon as I arrive and I'll write you every day," she promised. "At least a short note. And I won't be gone more than a few weeks at the most."

Her mother held Ina close to her. "Please be careful!"

"I will," she promised, drawing away from the distraught woman and picking up one of her suitcases. "I must go now."

So she was finally on her way. When the cab driver heard she was going to Austria, he talked dolefully about some bad landslides that had taken place there in the past few days. Ina confessed she had missed the news stories and doubted that they had taken place near St. Anton.

She arrived at the airport in good time to take her seat on the jet for Paris. And she settled back relaxed in the knowledge that the express train to Zurich and St. Anton would be waiting when she left the Paris airport to take her on her final leg of the trip to Marta's chalet in the Tyrol country.

The overseas flight was calm and uneventful and arrived in Paris right on schedule. She had no trouble getting through customs and immigration, taking a taxi to the proper railway station and boarding the express train with time to spare. She'd taken a compartment and at once settled down to have a good sleep. By the time the train halted at the St. Anton station late that afternoon, she was feeling rested.

A porter came to help her with her luggage when she stepped off the sleek train at the small railway station, and a seven-piece band was playing on the platform. The music was lively and in the polka tradition, exactly what a tourist might expect in Austria. There were a number of people getting off as well, most of them young couples arriving for skiing.

There was a healthy covering of pure white snow all around and the air was crisp and pleasant. She pulled her lynx-lined cloth coat tightly around her and enjoyed her first glimpse of this winter wonderland. Representatives of the various resort hotels were seeking out their people. She waited to see someone from Marta arrive and began to worry that they'd forgotten she was coming. Or perhaps they'd gotten the day wrong.

She continued waiting on the cold station platform as the train pulled away with a shrill whistle and a clatter of the car wheels. By this time most of the crowd had vanished to journey to one or other of the hotels in the busses provided.

One of the local railway porters came and tipped his cap to her. "May I assist Madame?" he wanted to know.

"Yes," she said. "I wish to go to the chalet of Marta Landen. Do you know it?"

"But of course," the porter said. "Can I get you a taxi?"

"I wish you would," she said. "I'm afraid they've forgotten about my coming. It's cold waiting here."

"One minute, young lady," the porter said and hurried off to the other end of the platform.

Not too long afterward an ancient taxi came chugging up in the snowy road before her and a thin, elderly man with a large drooping mustache loaded her baggage into its trunk and held out the rear door for her to enter.

In the wide back seat of the old car she leaned forward

to tell the driver, "I wish to go to Marta Landen's chalet."

The old man was already behind the wheel. "Yes, Madam," he said and started the motor.

She enjoyed the drive. They skirted the village with its quaint houses and imposing resort hotels. And she saw one of the Russian-type churches common in Austria with its support steeples crowned with what looked like huge artistic onions. To the left there rose spectacular peaks capped with snow. It was a land of white, blue and green, and in the enjoyment of its beauty she forgot for a few minutes that she'd not been met.

"Ahead is the castle!" the driver told her.

And she saw it set on a hillside like some fantastic fairy story castle. This was no ordinary chalet but a giant graystone fortress whose tall turrets challenged the blue sky above. Certainly Marta lived in surroundings as luxurious as a movie set.

They reached the entrance of the castle with its arched oaken door decorated with black wrought iron. The taxi driver unloaded her things and she paid him. At the same time the door opened and a gray-haired male servant with a slight stoop bowed to her.

She said, "I'm Ina Sperling. Your mistress is expecting me."

The old man's pinched face showed surprise. "Madame Leopold expected you?"

"Yes." She was getting impatient.

The servant stepped back. "Please enter," he said nervously. "I take you to the library. Mr. Leopold is there."

Ina was finding her reception at the castle a bit bewildering. But she followed the old servant along a gloomy corridor with a high ceiling to an open doorway. There the servant entered and crossed to a desk in the center of the library at which a stocky gray-haired man with a large Roman nose was sitting absorbed in some papers.

The old servant cleared his throat. "Sir, a Miss Ina Sperling is here. She says the mistress expected her."

The man at the desk showed surprise on his lined face as he glanced up. In a pleasant, cultured voice, he said,

"Really?" And he rose and came over to her. "Miss Sperling?"

"Yes," she said, increasingly baffled. "I've come to see your wife. Marta sent for me. I'm her niece by marriage."

David Leopold suddenly showed recognition. "Of course! I had completely forgotten! Forgive me! You are the journalist from America come to discuss her book with her."

"Yes," she said, relieved that he knew about her.

"I'm so sorry we had no one at the train to meet you," Leopold apologized. Then he told the servant, "Hans, take Miss Sperling's luggage up to the gray room on the third floor." As the old servant bowed and left, Marta's husband turned to her again. "I regret Marta is not here to greet you."

"I can see her later," Ina said.

"Let me take your coat," David Leopold said and went behind her to help her remove it. He put the coat on a nearby chair and said, "Now do sit down so I may have a serious talk with you."

"Thank you," she said. "I'm terribly impressed by this castle. It's overwhelming."

"Too large and expensive for us these days," the gray-haired man said. "Marta has had several offers for it by the hotel people and I'm sure she'll eventually sell it to them for conversion. The winter visitors to the area grow in numbers every year."

"You must have fine skiing here," she said.

"We do. The best," was David Leopold's reply. He hesitated and then said, "This is really a most awkward situation."

Suddenly she knew something was very wrong, that she was on the brink of some frightening revelation. Her nerves tensed. She stared at the man's worried face.

"What is it?" she asked.

"There is a good reason for my not having sent someone to pick you up at the station," David Leopold went on. "The house has been in a state of upset."

"Oh?"

"Yes," he went on nervously. "The truth of the matter is my wife is no longer here."

"No longer here!" she echoed.

"That is how it is," the stocky man in the expensively cut dark suit said. He touched a finger nervously to his tie.

Ina stared hard at him. "I don't follow you."

"I'll try to explain," David Leopold said. "We had a party here for a few friends on New Year's Eve. It has been a custom with us for some years. While the dancing was going on, my wife vanished."

"Vanished?"

"Yes," he said with a grave look. "Without a trace. She didn't even take her wrap with her. We searched the house completely and I checked with various friends. We discovered nothing. Marta had vanished as if she'd never been here."

She was shocked. "And you haven't heard from her since?"

"Not a word," David Leopold said sadly. "So now you can understand why you were forgotten. Marta mentioned your coming but in the strain of all this it slipped my mind."

"No wonder," she said.

"We're all in a state of confusion," the gray-haired man told her.

"What about the police"

"I waited a few hours, not knowing what her disappearance might mean and hoping she would turn up at the house of one of our friends. When this didn't happen I notified the authorities."

"What do they say?"

David Leopold sighed and sank down in the chair behind the broad mahogany desk. He said, "They are just as baffled as we are here."

"Was there any warning of this? Had she complained of being ill? Or had there been a quarrel?" Ina queried him.

"Nothing," he sighed. "No hint of her vanishing. Just nothing. And yet she has gone."

"Have the police any theory?"

"No. They suggested a suicide. That she might have gone to the stream beyond us in the hills. But it is too well frozen over for that to be easy. And a search there produced no signs of her having been there. In any case there was no reason for Marta to take her life."

"She cabled me only two weeks ago," Ina said, "and invited me here. She even told me the plane and train to take. She must have been expecting to see me."

The gray-haired man nodded sympathetically. "Without any question she was expecting you here. She was very excited about the book and she hoped you would do the actual writing of it."

"I put off a lot of work back in the United States to come here and help her with it," Ina said, still shocked. "What do you think happened?"

He shook his head. "All of us have tried to think of some explanation. The best we can come up with is possible amnesia."

"But you say she hadn't been ill?"

"No. But she could have been stricken by the amnesia without any warning," the old man pointed out.

"I suppose so."

"It seems the most likely answer. She may have had some sort of mental blackout and wandered off. She may have taken a train to Vienna and lost herself somewhere in the city. Or she could be at one of the resorts. There are so many."

Ina frowned. "But you say she had no luggage or any special clothing for outdoors?"

"No. That is why it strikes me that it had to be amnesia. In such cases the victims don't feel the cold and they usually later manage to get suitable clothing or have it given to them by some acquaintance they make."

"I'm sorry to be intruding at such a time!" Ina apologized.

"You are an invited guest," David Leopold said. "We can't blame you for being here. And I'm sure Marta would want you given a warm welcome."

"What am I to do?" she worried. "My work was all to be with her."

"Wait a few days," David Leopold said. "I have a strong feeling that she will turn up. Either the police will locate her or she'll come out of her mindless state and return on her own."

"Isn't that too much to hope for?"

"The police claim this happens every day. Missing persons recover their memories and return to their families."

"And they think this may happen with Marta?"

"Yes."

Ina said, "But if your wife is wandering around in a mental fog, I'd expect someone to see her and recognize her. She is a very famous movie star."

David Leopold's expression turned to one of sadness. "She is not a big star anymore. This once was true but today she can walk the streets of almost any city without being recognized. She belongs to the past. That irks her a great deal."

"I hadn't realized," she said.

"I think that was why she hoped to write her autobiography," Marta's husband went on. "She felt it would give her notoriety and a new public."

"Would it have worked?" she asked.

"I don't know," he replied worriedly. "I tried to talk her out of the idea." He made an extravagant gesture with his right arm. "We have no need of the possible profits."

Ina said, "I was to have all the profits of the book. She told me this in her letter."

"Really?" David Leopold said. "That doesn't surprise me. I know that she was only interested in the book as a medium to get herself back on the screen once more."

"She has had such an interesting history."

David Leopold's eyes widened. "You think so?"

"I do," she said. "And her early days with the Nazi leaders could have made one of the really sensational sections."

The old man seemed mildly surprised. "You feel that?"

"I would never have come all this way if I hadn't," Ina assured him.

"Of course I haven't given it any thought," he confessed.

"I understand."

"Marta was so looking forward to your visit," David Leopold went on. "She was anxious to have you know Gretchen."

"And I want to meet my cousin. It will be the first time."

"Naturally," the gray-haired man said.

"How is Gretchen taking her mother's disappearance?"

"Very well," he replied. "But then Gretchen is not easily touched. She is not the sentimental type. Still, it has been a dreadful strain on her."

"It would have to be."

"And our son, Claude, is greatly distressed," David Leopold said worriedly. "He refuses to believe that Marta left here on her own. He fears she may have been murdered."

She gave him a frightened look. "Do you think that's possible?"

"If you wish to take everything into consideration, I suppose it is," David Leopold said. "Though neither the police nor myself have felt this to be the case as yet. The general opinion is that she wandered off."

"Who would want to kill her?"

"Some insane person," he said. "The wealthy always attract madmen, and we are obviously wealthy. Or perhaps someone who knew her as a star and had some mental breakdown. Not a pleasant thing to consider. I refuse to give the theory credence."

"Has your son any special reason for feeling as he does? Were there ever any murder threats?"

"None."

"Or murders in the area?"

"None that I know of," David Leopold said. "I think Claude's concern has made him speculate wildly."

"Still it is a dreadful situation," Ina said, staring at the elderly man.

"I'm sorry you have been involved in it," David Leopold

said. "It is very unfortunate. You must be weary from your long journey. I'm sorry to have kept you here talking so long when you must be anxious to rest."

"I'm all right," she said. "Aside from the shock of this."

"When you have had time to rest, you must meet the others of our family," the gray-haired man said. He pressed a button on his desk and rose. "Hans will see you to your room. We usually gather in the drawing room before dinner. Please come down and join us if you feel well enough."

"Thank you," she said. Her mind was reeling with all that she had learned and she hadn't yet been able to properly sort it out.

Hans came noiselessly into the library and David Leopold ordered him to take her up to her room. She thanked Marta's husband again and followed the servant upstairs. The endless hallways and broad stairways impressed her as did the high ceilings and ornate décor of the old castle.

She followed Hans up to the third floor and he opened a door not far from the landing and showed her into a huge bedroom decorated in gray. The fourposter bed had a canopy of shining gray silk and the walls and drapes at the windows were a different shade of gray. The furniture was of period design and upholstered in gray satin. And even the rug which covered most of the hardwood floor was of a gray background with a red and yellow floral pattern in it.

The old servant said, "There is a buzzer, Miss. On the wall by the bed. It connects directly to the kitchen. If you wish anything just press it and a maid will come."

"Thank you for telling me," she said.

"Yes, Miss," Hans said and bowed and went out, closing the door after him.

For the first time since she'd arrived at the castle she was alone. She stood very still for a moment in the room with a ceiling so high it seemed to vanish in the shadows. Her bags had been placed neatly on stands at the foot of the bed. Hans was apparently a well-trained servant.

She crossed slowly to the bags and was about to open

one of them when she heard a scraping sound from behind her, as if wood was being drawn across wood. The odd sound made her stiffen and a chill of fear surged through her. She was at once filled with the eerie feeling that she was being spied on; that hostile eyes were watching her from some hidden place.

Her face pale, she wheeled around and stared at the paneled wall. She'd almost expected to see someone standing there. But the room seemed to be empty except for herself. Yet she had heard that odd noise and she was experiencing the sensation of being watched. It was very strange.

She stood there for long minutes, staring in the direction from which she felt the sound must have come. Then with a feeling of deep frustration she turned to the nearest of the suitcases again and began unpacking it. But the weird sensation of being spied upon continued!

Marta Landen had vanished! It seemed impossible and yet it had happened. And she had vanished only a short time before Ina's arrival. Could it mean that Marta had changed her mind about doing the frank autobiography? Perhaps someone had changed her mind for her—someone who did not relish their guilty secrets being betrayed.

Ina had not felt like suggesting this to Marta's loyal husband, but it could well be that the screen star's lurid past had caught up with her. But where could she have gone to? How had she been so neatly whisked away? David Leopold claimed it had happened during a New Year's Eve party for a few friends. And she assumed it must have happened well along in the evening when Marta's absence would not be immediately noticed.

Her husband had offered the amnesia theory and it could be the answer, in which case it was not a matter of secret enemies dealing with her but of a disease which had finally made itself apparent. Yet Ina felt this was far from a satisfactory explanation.

Ina was sure that Marta Landen had intended to go through with the autobiography, otherwise she wouldn't have sent for her as she had. Perhaps there was a small chance that she'd changed her mind and decided to postpone the venture. But if that were so she could have simply made this clear. There would be no need for her to vanish or deliberately hide to avoid a meeting.

With these troubled thoughts Ina finished her unpacking. The strange uneasiness which she'd felt previously was still with her. It was a feeling that things were not right in the old castle and that she was being spied on. It was a very unpleasant position to find herself in and almost matched her mother's most dire predictions.

She had cabled home on landing in Paris and would write a note to her mother before going to bed. She hardly knew what she'd write. It seemed that she should remain in the castle for a short while to see what happened. Yet if she told of Marta's disappearance, her mother would be completely upset and expect her to return home at once. She decided it might be better not to mention it for a little.

She took a shower in the modern bathroom adjoining her bedroom. It was obvious that Marta had converted one of the large closets of the big room into this latest-style bathroom. Ina then changed into a dark green dress which she felt might be suitable for the evening. It had a long skirt and a laced front with an insert of white.

Then she ventured out into the murky atmosphere of the wide corridor. The dimensions of the castle were overwhelming to someone used to living in a New York apartment. She started down the first of the stairways, her hand on the bannister. Tapestries had been hung at intervals along the wall to give some decoration and she noted that they were rich in color and expensive-looking.

She finally reached the lower hallway and hesitated. She heard no voices and saw no one. After a moment she decided to try the room to the left of the stairs. She moved across the hardwood floor to the wide entrance door and saw that it was a music room. In one corner of the big room there sat a grand piano with a violin case resting on it. And in the opposite corner there was a large organ with its seat a distance up from the floor and reached by three steps.

The arched windows of the big room were narrow and had stained glass at the top and plain glass below. There was a fine Persian rug on the floor, and the other divans, chairs and tables in the room were all period pieces and in good condition.

She was standing there absorbed by what she saw when someone came up beside her. She turned to find herself looking at a handsome young man in his late twenties with curly black hair and large, expressive black eyes.

He said, "May I introduce myself? I am Claude Leopold."

"The violinist," she said. "Of course now I recognize you. I've seen your photos."

He nodded. "And you are Ina Sperling from New York."

"Yes."

Marta's adopted son looked troubled. "You came here at my mother's request and now she is no longer here."

"So your father told me," Ina said. "I'm shocked."

"So are we all," the young man said gravely. "I had only been here a few days when it happened."

"It's so strange!"

Claude Leopold sighed. "I don't quite believe it yet. The castle is like a ghost house without her. She was the life of it. As you probably realize, my father is shattered by what happened."

"I had a short talk with him," she said. "I know he is very upset. How could he not be?"

The young man's sharp eyes searched her face. "It must be extremely unpleasant for you. You have come so far to find a situation like this."

"I wasn't in any way prepared for it," she admitted. "Marta seemed so anxious to get at her memoirs. What do you think has happened?"

"At the best she is mentally ill and has wandered off," the young man said. "At the worst someone may have murdered her."

"You don't think there's any possibility she might have become nervous about setting down her life story and decided to vanish for a while. At least until I return to America."

"I've thought of that," Claude agreed. "But it doesn't fit in with the things she said before her disappearance. She seemed happy and excited about the proposed book. She felt it would bring her back into the public eye again and renew her career."

"And so it might have," Ina said.

"If she believed that, she'd surely not vanish just as you were due to arrive," the young man said.

"I suppose not," Ina replied in a troubled tone. "This is such a large old place. I suppose she could be somewhere in it without others being aware of it."

"That's a real possibility," the violinist agreed. "Especially if, as my father thinks, she's had an attack of amnesia. She might be hiding somewhere in the castle without any real motive for doing so."

"Have you made a search?"

"A fairly thorough one. But we could still have missed her. It's a big place. They claim there are many secret passages. She could move about without us being aware of it."

"It's frightening," she said with a tiny shiver.

"I know," he said quietly. "Marta means a great deal to me. She adopted me when I was a child and I have grown up to think of her as my real mother, just as I look upon David as my father."

"He seems a fine man," Ina said.

"One of the finest I have ever known," Claude assured her. "He adores Marta and has always been gentle to her. There was no trouble there."

"I'm sure there wasn't, she said.

"Thanks to Marta I have a career in music," the young man went on. "And David is the manager of her affairs. She rescued us both from the concentration camps. She's a fine human being no matter what anyone may say about her."

She stared at the young man. "Has she been criticized?"

He shrugged gloomily. "Every so often one of the sensational magazines runs a story on her being an associate of Hitler and his gang. I doubt if anyone believes the stories, but they worried Marta."

"I knew there was quite a lot of that after the Second World War," she said. "I went through a lot of material on her before I came over here. But I sort of thought the smear campaign against her had ended."

"Perhaps in America," Claude said bitterly, "but not over here. They dig these things up again whenever there is no currently exciting story."

"What will they make of her disappearance?" she worried.

Claude frowned. "So far my father has been able to keep the news confined strictly to the local police authorities. But how long he can manage that is anybody's guess."

"They'll be bound to make the most of it," she prophesied.

"Without a question," Claude said.

She gazed about the ornate music room. "I can see that you were brought up in an atmosphere of music," she said.

"Yes," David agreed. "Marta always played the piano very well. When I was a youngster she had the patience to play for me as I did my exercises. It was she who realized I had a true talent for the violin."

"And there is a built-in organ as well," Ina said.

"She purchased that only a few years ago," the young man recalled. "And she seemed to get true pleasure from it. She alternated between it and the piano. But I think she was better on the piano."

Ina asked him, "Is that your violin on the piano?"

The young man looked sad. "Yes. On the morning before Marta vanished she played for me as I went over a few favorite tunes. It was like the old days, though she insisted she wasn't good enough to accompany me anymore. I felt she was."

"She and you were the only musicians in the house?"

"Yes," he said. "David enjoys music but he doesn't play."

"This entire business must be very hard on him," Ina said.

The young man sighed. "You may be sure of it. The truth is that David has never been a completely healthy person since his ordeal in the concentration camp. I'm sure he's still haunted by it."

"After so long?"

"Yes. As an adult it would be bound to be more terrifying and trying on him than it was for me; I was still a child and I only vaguely remember those days. Very little of it seems real to me now. It's more like a terrible dream. But for David, I'm certain it's much different. Marta told me he often finds it difficult to sleep.

"He suffers from insomnia?"

"Regularly," the handsome Claude said. "I was not aware of it, since I'm away a lot. But Marta said it had always been a problem for him since those days and lately it has been getting worse."

She said, "It sounds as if he really needed Marta. She understood him well."

"You have no idea how much he relied on her," Claude said. "He is putting on a good front for the time being. But I'm afraid if Mother doesn't soon show up, he'll collapse."

Ina stared at him. "You think he's that tense?"

"I do," the young man said solemnly.

"What about Gretchen?"

At the mention of his sister's name the young man showed a hint of anger. He said, "She's no help."

"I should think she would be. My uncle was her father. So she is my cousin."

David studied her hard. "You don't seem much like her."

"No?"

"No," he said emphatically. He then looked somewhat embarrassed as he went on to add, "Don't think I'm prejudiced, but Gretchen and I don't get along too well."

"I'm sorry," she said. "I didn't know."

The young man glanced out toward the hallway. "You'll be seeing her soon. It's a wonder she hasn't been down before this. She never misses before-dinner drinks."

There was a note of bitterness in his words which suggested a lot to Ina. She recalled that the mention Marta had made of her daughter in her letter had not been altogether clear. And Ina knew her own mother had suggested there was bound to be a conflict between Marta and her daughter if the girl planned a stage and film career. Marta, her mother had predicted, would be bound to resent competition even from her own flesh and blood.

She asked, "How is Gretchen taking this?"

"Stoically," the young man said in a grim tone.

"Having her mother vanish this way can't have been easy for her," she said.

Claude met her eyes with a strange look of his own. He said, "You don't understand how it was between those two."

"No. I don't."

"Well," he said, "You'll find out. Perhaps we should go on to the drawing room. "The others are likely there now."

She followed him from the music room and along a corridor which led under the broad stairway. There another broad entrance led to the drawing room. It was the largest of all the rooms Ina had seen and it was dominated by two immense chandeliers whose cut glass shimmered with light. A huge full-length portrait of Marta as a young woman in her twenties was on the wall opposite the entrance and met your eyes as soon as you started to enter the immense room.

"Your mother!" Ina gasped, halting a little as she studied the painting from the vantage point of the entrance.

The young violinist paused with her. "Yes," he said. "She looks lovely in it, doesn't she?"

"Yes. It captures all her beauty."

"She still looks much as she did then," Claude said, studying it with Ina. "At least she did when I last saw her on New Year's Eve. She was surely older and her face had thinned with age, but she had that fine bone structure which stood by her."

"I'm sure of that," Ina agreed.

"So much for Mother," Claude said in a taut voice. "Father and Gretchen are down at the other end of the room by the sideboard."

She went further into the room and saw that this was so. The two turned their way as she and Claude walked down the length of the big room. Ina noted that David Leopold had changed to black tie and dinner jacket. Standing by him with a glass in her hand was a slim, lovely blonde who resembled Marta in a startling way in everything else but her hair color.

David Leopold came to greet them with a smile on his lined, weary face. "So glad you decided to join us, Miss Sperling. I want you to meet my daughter, Gretchen."

Ina advanced toward the blonde girl with a smile and hand held out. "How nice to finally meet you, cousin!"

Gretchen eyed her sullenly. "So you're the one from America." She made no effort to take Ina's hand, and from her slightly slurred words it was evident that she had been drinking a good deal.

To make the best of a situation Ina said, "Yes. I'm your cousin from the States. I'm only sorry your mother isn't here."

"I'll bet you are," the blonde girl said almost sneeringly.

David Leopold looked upset and interposed at once to say, "You mustn't mind Gretchen. She is very upset about Marta's disappearance."

The pretty blonde turned to him at this and laughed harshly. "Me upset? You must be joking! I don't care! And I'm the only one who really knows what happened to her!"

There was a tense moment of silence among the little group. Then Ina said, "What did happen to her?"

Gretchen took a sip of her drink and gave Ina a mocking glance. "The ghost got her! Who else?"

The blonde girl eyed her incredulously. "There's only one. He glides down the slopes almost every night. You just have to be at the right spot at the right time to see him."

Still bewildered, she asked, "See who?"

"The ghost of Karl Bruck," Gretchen informed her. "The natives say he haunts the place."

"Gretchen!" David Leopold called out in a tormented voice.

"I forgot," she jeered at him over her glass. "For a moment I didn't remember how sensitive you are about that."

"I say you didn't forget!" David Leopold said and swung away so that his back was to them all.

Claude took over the situation. Turning to Gretchen he said, "Since you have said so much, why not tell her it all?"

Gretchen eyed him bleakly. "You tell her!" she suggested.

"I will," the young man said. "First, what would you like to drink, Ina?"

"Nothing for the moment," she said.

"Then we don't need to stand so near the bar," the curly-haired man said, taking her by the arm and moving her away from the sideboard. They strolled a little distance up the room, halting not far from the wide entrance.

She said, "I didn't seem to make a very good impression on Gretchen."

Claude shook his head. "Nothing personal," he assured her. "She's been drinking too much today and when she drinks too much she's always incoherent and nasty."

"I see," she said.

"You don't," he corrected her. "Or at least not all of it. It happens that Gretchen didn't get along with her mother. There was very bad blood between them."

"I've been suspecting that."

"There are good and sufficient reasons," the handsome young violinist went on briskly. "Some of the fault lies with Gretchen and some of it with our mother."

CHAPTER THREE

Ina was only too well aware of the tension in the high-ceilinged drawing room. Where there had been silence before there was sheer consternation now. David Leopold's weary face had gone pale and even the handsome Claude looked slightly shocked. Gretchen, seeming to enjoy the scene she had caused, watched them all with a tiny, self-satisfied smile.

It was David Leopold who broke the tension first. He turned to the pretty blonde girl and reprimanded her, "We understand you, Gretchen, but your cousin is not prepared for your weird nonsense."

Gretchen showed no hint of apology. "I say what I think," was her reply.

In his slightly accented English, Marta's husband turned to Ina with embarrassment. He said, "I must ask you not to take what Gretchen says too seriously. She has some very strange ideas."

Ina said, "I'm always interested in hearing fresh opinions."

Claude Leopold spoke up bitterly, saying, "I'm afraid Gretchen is more likely to offer you local gossip. Old wives' tales straight from the servants' quarters."

Gretchen spoke directly to Ina. "They're both trying to cover up something that can't be covered up. When I said the ghost got my mother, that's exactly what I meant."

"What ghost?" Ina asked.

"So?"

"So Gretchen is not exactly heartbroken by what has happened. She'd probably cheer if she were sure she'd never see Mother alive again."

"It's that bad?"

"I'm afraid so," Claude said.

"It's very sad."

"Yes, it is," he agreed, looking back down at the opposite end of the room where the other two were still standing. "Especially as she particularly likes to upset my father."

"What did she mean by saying the ghost got Marta?"

Claude smiled without humor. "It's her idea of being clever. You know that my father was not the first man in Marta's life?"

"Yes."

"I don't consider that of importance," the young man went on. "Marta took both David and me in at a time when we needed help. I'm sure she loved David just as she's shown devotion to me. But he is still badly upset whenever there is a reference to what went on before. When she was linked with those Nazis."

"I've read about that."

David's eyes were pained. "Then you must have encountered the name of Karl Bruck?"

"Yes."

"Rumor has it that it was he who bought this castle and set Marta up in it. She has another version of the story. She says it was money she earned from her first German film successes. But since Karl Bruck was the one at the head of the department passing on these films, he must have had a good part in those early hits."

"And?" she questioned him.

"And so Karl Bruck once lived here for short periods with Marta. He enjoyed the skiing at St. Anton and often went out on the slopes here. Gossip has it that his phantom still can be seen on the hills on moonlit nights. A ghostly figure on skis!"

"And it was the ghost of Karl Bruck she meant had captured Marta?" Ina asked.

"Yes," the young man said grimly. "Not that she really believes it, but it made a smart comment. She also knew it would hurt David and she enjoys taunting him."

"You make her sound like a very unpleasant person."

"She is."

"Too bad."

"You think so?"

Ina nodded. "Yes. She is so attractive. She has all of Marta's good looks, and her blonde hair is both a contrast and interesting."

"Marta had great talent," Claude said. "Gretchen has very little. At least she's not shown much so far."

"It's not easy to be the daughter of a famous star," she told him.

"I realize that," the young violinist said. "But if she'd been less aggressive about having a theatre career, Marta would have helped her. But when she made it plain to Mother she hoped to be a bigger star than her, the seeds for trouble were sown."

Ina gave him a knowing glance. "I've heard that Marta could also be difficult enough when she liked."

His brow furrowed. "You met her once, didn't you?"

"Years ago in Hollywood," she said. "I was only a child at the time. I only have a blurred memory of her as being very beautiful and somewhat cold."

"Your mother took you there?"

"Yes."

"Were your mother and Marta friendly?" Claude asked.

"Not too," she admitted.

Claude said, "That could explain your impression of Marta. You were guided in your view of her by your mother."

"Perhaps to a degree," she said reluctantly. "But from other sources, people who knew Marta, I've had some opinions of her. And most of them agreed she was temperamental."

The young violinist gestured impatiently with his free

hand as he continued to hold his glass in the other. He said, "Maybe they were right. I think more kindly of Marta than most because she was a mother to me in the truest sense of the word. I owe all that I am to her."

Ina regarded him with sympathy. "I think it is right and proper that you should think as you do. But I also wonder if the picture in your mind of her is a completely true one. I'd be inclined to say it wasn't. That in your own way you're just as biased in your views as Gretchen is in her's."

At this moment David Leopold came up with Gretchen at his side and told them, "I'm afraid I'll have to break up this interesting tête-à-tête. Dinner is waiting for us."

They dined in a long, rather narrow room. The food and service were excellent. The elderly Hans presided over the servants and saw that everything was right. Conversation at the dinner table was not easy, and Gretchen's almost continual antagonism to anything said was the chief culprit.

After dinner they returned to the drawing room for coffee and brandy. David Leopold saw everyone seated by a circular coffee table with a marble top and Hans came with a tray to serve them.

Ina found herself seated next to Gretchen, with David and Claude across from them but far enough away to make talk difficult. So she was left to the devices of the sarcastic girl.

Fortunately Gretchen, in an expensive blue halter dress which showed a lot of her bosom and almost all her back, now seemed in a better mood. No doubt the meal and coffee had helped to sober her. An expensive ruby and diamond ring sparkled on one of her fingers as she put down the coffee cup in its saucer.

Looking at Ina with a somewhat penitent expression on her lovely face, she said, "I drink too much."

Ina showed a small smile. "Do you?"

"You know it," the other girl said. "You heard me talking in the library. When I'm drinking I'm nasty."

"Thank you for the warning."

The blonde girl was staring at her intently and Ina could now see the shadows of blue under the young woman's eyes. Already she was beginning to show evidence that her hard drinking was ruining her beauty.

Gretchen said, "You are my father's niece."

"Yes."

"I can see his looks in you," Gretchen said. "I have some snapshots of him still. Mother tried to get her hands on them. If she had, I'd never have seen them again. But she didn't get them!"

Ina was surprised. "Didn't she want you to know what your father looked like?"

"Not her," Gretchen said with disgust. "She claimed she didn't want any reminders of my father around. It upset her. What it amounted to was she intended to be the dominant figure in my life. She didn't want me to even have a clear memory of my father."

"That's very strange."

"My mother was a very strange person," Gretchen said.

"You say "was" as if she weren't still alive," Ina pointed out.

"Who knows that she is?" the blonde girl replied.

"But surely everyone hopes that she is," Ina protested.

Gretchen smiled grimly. "I won't offer any comments on that. It sort of spoils everything for you, doesn't it?"

"Yes."

"Are you going to stay a while?"

"Your father suggested that I should," she said.

Gretchen looked disgusted. "He's not my father, as you very well know. Marta tried to force that down my throat along with all the other things. I refused to call him Father even as a child."

"He is your stepfather and I'm sure he cares for you," she said.

"Don't be too sure," the blonde girl said curtly. "He and Claude band together against me. They always have. And my mother preferred to be on their side."

"I think you're probably exaggerating things."

Gretchen sat back in her chair with a grim smirk. "You don't know much about it."

"I'll admit that."

"Then don't offer opinions!"

"I'm sorry," she said. "There is one thing. You made a very strange statement earlier before dinner. You said a ghost was responsible for your mother's disappearance. What did you mean?"

"I meant Karl Bruck's ghost," Gretchen said. "He was the famous Nazi she was mixed up with. They claim his ghost haunts this house and the ski slopes near here. I say he came back to claim her because she was going to write that book about her life. It would have meant her telling about him. I don't think he'd like that. Not even as a ghost."

"That's pretty far-fetched, isn't it?" Ina said.

"I don't know. If he didn't do it, maybe some of his friends are still around and decided to get her out of the way before she wrote the truth about them."

"You mean Nazis?"

"I guess you'd have to be a Nazi to be a friend of Karl Bruck," Gretchen said with another of her cold smiles. "Don't think there aren't any left."

"I have no idea," she said. "Did your mother ever mention them?"

Mother?" Gretchen raised a shapely eyebrow. "You must be joking. She would never even admit to having known a Nazi, in spite of the newspaper stories about her younger days. I don't know why. She wasn't fooling anyone."

"Certainly not you."

"Especially not me," Gretchen said.

Ina felt she could no longer resist asking, "Why do you hate your mother so?"

Gretchen's slim hands clenched the arms of her chair. "Does there have to be a reason? Don't some people resent others just by instinct? A matter of chemistry, I understand."

"It's more than chemistry in this case, I'm sure."

"Ask the others!" Gretchen said bitterly. "Ask them who interfered every time I had a film or stage offer? Who was afraid I was trading on their famous reputation? And who tried to steal every man who showed any interest in me!" With this delivered, the blonde girl got quickly up from her chair and stalked out of the drawing room.

David Leopold at once rose and came over to sit by Ina solicitously. "I hope Gretchen wasn't too unpleasant to you," he said.

"I think perhaps I upset her."

"I'd say that is most unlikely," the elderly man said.

Claude was now standing near her and he stared down at her with an understanding look. "Just don't let her frighten you away from here. I think that's what she wants."

"But why?" Ina asked, baffled.

"That might take quite a time to explain," the young violinist said. "I think you should remain here and see if Mother doesn't turn up. If she doesn't, I believe you should try and put her notes together and write the book as she intended it to be written."

"Were there notes?" she asked.

David nodded. "Yes, my wife has been jotting down items for some years now. Items around which to build her memoirs. I'm not at all sure what she did with them. I wondered if she had sent you any such material."

"No," she said. "I had only the letter in which she discussed her biography."

Claude Leopold said, "It shouldn't be too hard to search out the material from among her things."

His father seemed upset at this. "Not yet, Claude," he said. "I can't allow anything like that yet. It is my belief and my hope that your mother will return and then it will be plenty of time to go into this book business."

"Suppose she doesn't return," Claude said. "Suppose she is dead."

David Leopold's face was ashen. "I can't believe that. She will return. I know it!"

Claude gave her a special side lok to indicate the hopelessness of arguing with his father. He said, "Let us pray you are right."

"It hasn't been all that long," she said. "Only a few days."

50

David Leopold sighed deeply. "I keep asking myself what it means."

Ina said, "What were the exact circumstances of her vanishing? You didn't tell me."

The younger man was the first to answer. Still standing by her chair, he said, "It was just after the New Year came in. Marta sat at the piano and played for us to sing as the old year passed. Then she came over to me and kissed me on the cheek and told me that she knew this was going to be my year of biggest success. And I replied that I felt the same about her. You know, the sort of thing one says on those occasions."

"I know," she said.

Claude went on, "Next she left the music room in search of Father. I didn't see her after that."

David Leopold spoke up, "She came to me in the drawing room. I had been caught there by a bore telling a long-winded story and hadn't been able to get to the music room in time to join in signing with the others. She found me and we embraced and exchanged good wishes."

Ina said, "And then?"

"I don't remember too clearly," the older man worried. "It seems to be that it was just after that the phone call came for her."

Claude Leopold looked surprised. "What phone call, Father? You didn't say anything about a phone call before?"

The gray-haired man looked slightly flustered. "Didn't I? In my distress I must have forgotten. There was a call. One of the maids, I don't know which one, came and told her she was wanted on the phone. She took the call in the hallway. I remember joining her there just as she finished talking and I thought she looked pale. I asked her if she felt all right."

"What did she say?" Ina asked.

The old man frowned. "She said she was just a little tired. And she suggested that I should take a quick round of the house and make sure that our guests were enjoying themselves."

Claude said, "And you did?"

"Yes," his father replied. "I checked and discovered that some of them were leaving. I went to tell Marta so that she could say good night to them, but I couldn't find her. I at once assumed that she'd felt ill and decided to go up to bed. So I took over the duty of seeing our friends on their way."

"And afterward?" Ina said.

David Leopold gave her a troubled look. "Afterward I went up to our room and she was not there. It was then I began to worry and started a search of the house. I roused Claude who had gone to his room and told him what had happened."

"I couldn't believe it," the young man protested. "That Mother would vanish in the middle of the night that way. It didn't make sense."

"Still we were unable to find her in the house," David Leopold said sadly.

"Where was Gretchen?" Ina queried.

David Leopold looked embarrassed. "She had been to a party at the Post Hotel that afternoon. She drank too much and one of her friends booked a room for her there. She didn't return until the next morning. By that time her mother had been missing for hours."

Claude addressed his father. "Then the last time you actually saw her was in the hallway. After she'd taken that mysterious phone call."

"I wouldn't call it a mysterious phone call," the old man protested. "I didn't consider it of any consequence at the time."

"But you now say Mother seemed upset by it," Claude told him.

"I thought she looked weary or even ill, but I didn't connect it with the call," David Leopold said.

"Still it was after the call that she vanished," the young man said. "And you say she did seem upset."

David Leopold was now obviously nervous. "In my opinion it was merely some friend calling to wish her a happy new year. Someone who had missed the party."

"But you don't know that," Claude worried. "I wish you had told me about it then. And you should have mentioned it to the police."

The gray-haired man looked uneasy. "I see now that it was stupid of me. But until we went over it all just now I'd really forgotten about the call. When the police arrived here I was in such a state I could barely talk to them." He touched a hand to his temple. "You know how it is with me!"

"I'm sorry, Father," Claude said. "I didn't mean to condemn you. I only wanted to make it clear the phone call could have had importance."

David Leopold rose wearily from his chair. "If Marta does not soon return, I don't know what I'll do."

Claude at once went to him and patted him on the shoulder. "It is going to be all right. You will see. There has to be some good explanation for all this."

The old man's features had become agitated. "Just so long as she returns," he said with a tremor. "That is all I ask." And he went out of the room.

Ina was on her feet now. She said, "I shouldn't have asked so many questions. Blame it on my reportorial training. I'm afraid we've upset him badly."

Claude's handsome face showed sympathy. "You mustn't blame yourself. This is not your fault, any of it. And I'm glad you did start the questioning, otherwise I would never have learned about that phone call."

"Do you think it has all that importance? Your father could be right. It may have been only a friend."

"I don't know, but I'm going to try and find out," the young violinist said. "It might have been someone from Mother's past calling to warn her against doing the book. That could have been the reason she decided to vanish as she did."

"On such short notice? In the middle of the night?"

Claude shrugged. "Maybe whoever it was told her they wanted to talk to her about something. They might have said they'd come by in a car to pick her up."

"At that time of night?"

"New Year's Eve is a night of late happenings. It's also often a night when people think of old scores and sometimes decide to even them."

"You are very convincing," she admitted. "I'm almost ready to swing around to your point of view. The police should certainly be told about the call."

"I know." he said. "You can see now the scars the concentration camp left on my father. In a crisis he often becomes confused and frightened. It harks back to those days when he starved as he waited to be led to the gas chambers. That sort of memory dies hard and very slowly. For him the fear will always be not too far away like a cloud ready to come sweeping over him."

"Poor man!" she said.

Claude smiled bitterly. "I was in the same sort of place and being readied for an identical fate, but I was too young to be aware of the horror of it. It was like a strange adventure for me and so I came through it comparatively unscathed."

"I'm glad," she said.

"Thank you," he said. "This has been a very bad welcoming for you. But we shall try to do better. I'd like to show you the village and have you enjoy some of the skiing while we wait to see what is going to happen."

"I can't expect that of you," she said. "You are under this terrible strain."

"We mustn't allow it to completely crush us," he said. "Our only hope is to continue in a normal fashion and trust that my mother will come back."

"It isn't the same for me," she said. "I didn't know her. I only had that letter from her and the one meeting with her long ago."

"But you decided to come here."

"Her book offered me a challenge."

"I repeat that you should write it no matter what happens," Claude said.

"We'll decide later," she said. "Your father is opposed to us interfering with her private papers now, and I'd say he was quite right. If she returns and finds we've been prying into her notes, she is liable to be very upset."

"That's true," Claude said reluctantly. "But if the papers are valuable they should be given special care."

Ina pointed out, "We don't know just what notes exist. So it is hard to say. Better wait."

"Father seemed to have some idea she might have sent part of her material on to you," the young man said.

"I heard him mention that," she agreed. "Of course he is wrong."

"It's a strange business," Claude worried.

"You should make another search of the castle," Ina said. "If she had a mental collapse she could still be hiding somewhere in this big old place."

"I'll speak to Hans," the young man promised. "We'll look again tomorrow. Though I doubt if we'll have any luck."

"Which means she must have gone out into the night for some reason," she said. "And without even a coat to protect her from the cold."

"The phone call gives me other ideas," Claude said. "She might have been meeting someone who had a heated car. Someone who phoned to keep a rendezvous with her."

All at once Ina had a new picture of the situation. She had forgotten that Marta was inclined to play the field. Even though she was definitely an older woman, she was still attractive and had the glamor of her starring days to bolster her image. And while she might be very fond of her husband, it would not occur to her that she should have to remain completely faithful to him. There could be some other younger man who was courting her and who had called to make a New Year's Eve tryst with her.

She looked up at Claude gravely. "Is there a man?"

"Yes."

"Someone here in St. Anton?"

"Yes."

She hesitated. "You think she might have gone away with him?"

"It's possible. I didn't think of it until tonight. Now I'll have to look into the possibility."

55

"I didn't think of it," she said. "I think of her as I would my mother. As an older woman."

Claude looked grim. "Marta doesn't see herself that way. She sees herself as she was twenty-five years ago."

"Gretchen accused her of trying to steal men from her."

"It's possible," the young violinist said in an upset voice. "This time I won't find it easy to forgive her. She has no right to make my father suffer this way."

"You may be accusing her unjustly," she warned him.

"I hope so," he said. "I love Marta as well as any son could. But I love my father too."

Ina touched his arm. "Poor Claude," she whispered.

His expressive black eyes met hers and there was that magic spark of understanding between them. And without saying anything he took her by the arms and drew her close to kiss her. He held her to him as if seeking refuge and consolation in her close physical presence. And she didn't resist, since in the short time of their acquaintance she had come to like him and feel sympathy for him.

He looked at her solemnly. "I didn't mean to be brash."

She smiled. "You weren't. I'd like to hear you play one day soon."

"I'll be glad to," he said.

"Right now I'm suddenly exhausted," she told him. "I must go up and get some sleep."

"I'll see you upstairs," Claude said.

"No need," she protested.

"I'm going up anyway," he said.

They left the drawing room and went around the corridor to the stairway. Once again she was impressed by the size and elegance of the place. The lights had been almost all turned out and a deep silence cloaked the old castle. Claude said little as they made their way up to the third floor, and his good night at the door of her bedroom was restrained.

She went inside and closed the door and saw that the bed had been turned down for her and there was a nice log fire blazing in the fireplace. Some of her vague feelings of fear vanished before the warm cosiness of the room. No one could complain of the staff.

Slowly she prepared for bed with her thoughts still centered on the enigma of Marta Landen's disappearance. The evening had brought her a lot of fresh information, though she had no idea of its value. The most dramatic statement of all had been Gretchen's declaration that the ghost of Karl Bruck had returned to claim Marta.

The phantom of the slopes had come to take his own. It was amazing that people still remembered Karl Bruck and spoke of his avenging ghost a quarter-century after his death in that Berlin bunker. It showed what a power the man had been and how vicious a reputation he'd built for himself. He'd created an atmosphere of terror so strong that the simple locals were touched by his evil these long years after his death!

And Marta had surely been close to him. The photos that were public knowledge and the many articles and stories of that other era vouched for that. Ina thought back to the photo in the files of the New York Public Library. It had been a blurred reproduction but she remembered the man in SS uniform who had stood beside Marta as curiously insignificant looking, except for the monocle he wore.

But despite the superstition of the local people, Karl Bruck had been dead for twenty-five years or more and it seemed unlikely that his ghost had anything to do with the disappearance of Marta Landen. Just before the evening had ended, Claude had suggested a much more plausible explanation, that Marta might have kept a rendezvous with some man. But if that was the case why hadn't she returned? Once again the possibility of violence came into the picture. Had Marta been murdered and abandoned by some callous lover?

Naturally David Leopold refused to think of any such things in connection with his missing wife. His belief was that she'd suffered an attack of amnesia and was still wandering mindlessly somewhere. If that were true, why not somewhere in the dark hidden places of the old castle?

No matter what, the macabre incident had completely upset Ina's plans, and perhaps it would be a permanent upset. Claude kept suggesting that she write the book in any case, but that wouldn't be possible unless she had a reasonable amount of private material left by Marta. Otherwise the study would be superficial and not likely to attract a large audience.

With these thoughts uppermost in her mind Ina got into the canopied bed and turned out the lights. Outside a winter wind was blowing and its whistling about the graystone castle created an eerie sound. It was hard to settle down to sleep in these strange surroundings but she closed her eyes and tried.

After a little she sank into a dreamless sleep. She had no idea how long she'd been sleeping when she suddenly came awake with a start. She was certain someone had just walked across the room by the foot of her bed. She sat up in bed staring into the darkness, her heart pounding with fear of the intruder and yet not able to see anyone.

She tried to rationalize and convince herself that she must have been dreaming. But the conviction that there had been someone in the room still persisted. The wind outside continued to provide a mournful background to her fears and nervously she reached out for the bedside lamp and switched it on. The bedroom seemed empty.

But she was still not satisfied. She slipped out of bed, put on her robe and cautiously made her way to the bathroom and looked in through the doorway but could see no one in there. Then she tried the closets with the same result. Baffled but not yet convinced she had imagined the intruder, she went to the door leading to the corridor and opened it.

She gazed out into the shadows of the wide corridor and then slowly advanced outside. She made her way to the head of the stairway and touched a hand to the bannister. Then she decided she was behaving foolishly. She should return to her bedroom and go back to sleep again. It was, of course, easier to say than to do, but she must try.

With this resolution made, she was about to turn and go back when from far below there came a sound which froze her where she stood. Someone was in the music room playing the organ! The strains of a Wagnerian overture came booming up to her, sending an icy chill down her spine. Someone was playing the organ which only Marta played!

Fear distorted her pretty face at the thought of ghostly fingers on the keyboard of the organ and a ghostly figure seated at it. But at the same time she had a more optimistic thought. It could be that a confused Marta had returned to the castle and sat down at the organ. The eerie playing continued and Ina made up her mind to go all the way down to the music room and see who was there. But she was still torn by fear and so was slow to descend the stairs in the after-midnight darkness.

She encouraged herself by telling herself that when she reached the music room she would find Marta there. The film star would still be suffering from amnesia but would respond to medical treatment and all would be well. The first step in bringing about this happy denouement was to brave the darkness and go to that room from which the organ music still issued.

Reaching the lower foyer, she found the organ music now louder and more frightening than ever. Whoever was at the keyboard was playing in a strange, frantic manner. Ina started across to the music room but she never did get there. When she was a third of the way across a figure suddenly emerged from the shadows and confronted her.

In the near darkness she was only able to make out vaguely the face and figure of the ghostly creature. But one look was enough. She found herself staring at an elderly man with long, matted gray hair and a face terribly scarred so that the mouth was no more than an ugly gaping circle and one eye was shut. The other eye seemed alive with madness and a thin, hooked nose drooped over the ruined mouth!

Ina stumbled back with a terrified scream. As she did so the ghostly apparition snarled and came toward her with a shuffling gait. She turned and started back up the broad stairway with the phantom following. As she screamed out her fear again she knew he was catching up with her and in perhaps another moment she would be his victim.

And now the moment came and she felt his bony fingers grasp her by the ankle. She stumbled and gasped out her horror as she went toppling down the stairs.

CHAPTER FOUR

She was conscious of a racking pain in her head and bright lights invading the dark well into which she'd retreated. She blinked and looked up and saw that both David and Claude Leopold were kneeling by her anxiously.

"The bright lights," she murmured unhappily and shut her eyes to guard herself against them.

A hand was on her shoulder. "Ina, are you badly hurt?" Claude was asking her in a frightened voice.

"Let her be for a moment," David Leopold counseled his son in his deeper voice.

She knew she shouldn't be worrying them. They had troubles enough. It wasn't fair of her to be behaving so childishly. Using this self-rebuke as a stimulus she again opened her eyes and tried to endure the blinding lights.

"Where am I?" she asked, still confused.

"At the foot of the lower stairway," Claude said, his handsome face anxious. "You must have lost your footing and fallen most of the way."

"What were you doing down here in the middle of the night?" David Leopold wanted to know.

It all came back to her with frightening clarity. She raised herself on an elbow as she cried, "The man! The old man with the horrible face! Hideously scarred! He followed me up the stairs and tripped me!"

Claude and his father exchanged grave looks as if to question her words. Then Claude asked her, "Are you saying that you met someone who caused you to topple down the stairs?"

"Yes. I told you. A hideously scarred ghostly old man!" she said.

"Why did you come down here in the first place?" David Leopold asked, a puzzled look on his weary face.

"The organ," she said. "Someone was playing the organ!"

Claude stared at her. "Someone was playing the organ?"

"Yes," she said. "I heard it from the hallway upstairs and thought Marta might be back. So I came down here."

David Leopold frowned and then at once got up and left her to go off down the hall, probably to the music room. Meanwhile she was conscious of the look of disbelief on Claude's face.

The violinist said, "It sounds more and more as if you've suffered from a bad nightmare!"

"No. All of it happened!"

"I can't understand why the rest of us didn't hear the organ if it were being played. We came down because we heard you scream. But there was no hint of an organ playing."

"It was the organ that attracted me," she insisted.

"You're telling us a strange story," Claude warned her.

"I can't change it," she said, "for that is exactly what happened."

The older Leopold returned with a look of skepticism on his worried, lined face. He came to stand by her and then, as if delivering a sentence from the judge's stand, he said, "There's no sign of anyone being near the organ. The keyboard is locked just as we usually keep it."

She struggled to her feet. "No! You have to be wrong!"

"I'm afraid I'm not," the old man said gravely. "If you like, you can go and see for yourself."

Ina swayed slightly as if she might collapse again. Claude at once put an arm around her to bolster her and at the same time he said, "I still wonder why, if there was music, some of the others didn't hear it."

"I can't tell you that," she said. "But I know that I heard it!"

David Leopold looked alarmed. "If you did it must have been ghost music," he said. "I've already told you the organ is kept locked and it is locked now."

"What woke you in the first place?" Claude asked her. "You surely couldn't hear sounds from the music room in your bedroom!"

"There was someone in my room," she said.

"Who?" the older man demanded.

"I don't know. I just sensed someone being there. But when I got up to look, there was no one."

"And then?" Claude demanded.

"Then I decided whoever it had been might be in the hall, so I went out there. I ventured as far as the stairs and was about to turn back when I heard the organ music. And it was coming from the music room."

David Leopold's lined face showed impatience. He said, "I think the whole business can be explained by your having had a bad dream."

"It can't have been," she protested in frustration. "I felt that hand catch my ankle and I saw the old man's disfigured face!"

David Leopold was plainly angry. He said, "I refuse to stay up the rest of the night listening to these hysterical stories. I suggest the young lady return to her bed and we can better deal with this in the morning."

"Go on, Father," his son told him. And he remained with Ina as the older man mounted the stairs on his way back to his room.

Claude said, "Let me apologize for my father. He is old and very upset."

"I don't ask for an apology," she said unhappily. "I only ask to be believed."

The violinist said. "My main concern is whether or not you are hurt."

"Bruised a little, that's all," she said. And she felt it to be true, since the throbbing pain in her head caused by the fall had finally ceased.

"Then I'll turn out the lights," he said. "Fortunately we woke none of the servants." And he proceeded to turn out the lights and then return to her.

She stared at him. "You don't believe me!"

"I didn't say that."

"You don't have to," she complained. "It is plain enough in your manner."

He touched her elbow to guide her up the stairs. "As my father said, we can discuss it in the morning. We'll all be a lot calmer and more like ourselves then."

She began ascending the stairs with him at her side but still she was unhappy that her story was being brushed aside. "You think I panicked and made it all up."

"I think you shouldn't have come downstairs alone."

"There was no time to try and rouse anyone else," she lamented.

"That is what you should have done."

"But I heard the ghostly music," she persisted, "and I saw that horrible, ugly phantom!"

"Try and calm yourself," he advised her.

They were on the second landing and she turned to him and asked, "Don't you believe any of it?"

Claude answered in a patient voice, "I'm sure there has to be some basis for your upset. You're far too sensible a girl to just panic and make a scene. But I think we should wait until daylight to analyze just what it all means."

"Placating words!" she said angrily.

"Suppose they are," Claude said as they started the final flight of stairs to the third floor.

"I did hear the organ playing!"

"All right, you did!"

"If your father found it to be locked, someone must have locked it between the time I collapsed and he went to check on the organ. There wouldn't have been any great trick to that."

"I suppose not," Claude said guardedly.

"And I did meet that scarred man. I can even describe his face in detail to you."

"Don't try to now. It will only make it more difficult for you to get to sleep," he warned her.

"What I heard and saw may have a bearing on your mother's disappearance," she warned him.

"I know."

"Then why don't you do something about it instead of doubting my word?"

"Because first I must make certain investigations of my own," he replied. "If they suggest you've been telling us facts and not fancies, then I'll work out a plan of action."

"You mean my word isn't good enough?"

"I'm afraid not in this instance," Claude said as they reached her door. "I don't blame you for having nightmares, but don't try to live them out another time."

They had reached the door to her bedroom again and this time she felt them to be truly poles apart. She said a wretched good night and he asked whether there was anything else he could do. Her reply was to go into her bedroom and shut the door after her. Her bedside lamp was on and she slept with it on for the balance of the night.

When she got up the next morning she saw that the snowy countryside was bright with sunlight. It was a beautiful day and contrasted sharply with her own bleak feelings. She showered and dressed and was about to go downstairs when a knock came on her door. She opened it to find a thin young woman in a maid's uniform carrying a tray with breakfast on it.

Ina stood back to allow her to enter. She said, "I didn't know I was to have room service."

"Yes, Miss," the girl said in nearly perfect English. "It is how we do it here. Breakfast in the room. You can ring the kitchen if you wish it earlier." As she spoke she placed the tray on a table by the window and arranged the dishes for Ina.

Ina went over to join her and said, "You timed it very well."

"Yes, Miss," the maid bobbed politely. "If there is anything else, let me know."

She surveyed the heavy breakfast and shook her head. "I don't think that's likely."

"I have brought you coffee, Miss," the maid said. "You did not wish tea?"

"Not in the mornings," she said, seating herself at the table with a smile. "I like coffee to begin the day."

The maid nodded and said solemnly, "Coffee is good." There was an odd musical cadence to her way of speaking English which Ina found pleasing.

"Is it popular in Austria?"

"Oh, yes, Miss," the maid said. "We have many coffee houses here. They are a gathering place for people and we have many kinds of coffee. In some of the coffee houses newspapers are fastened to round poles and hung on racks. One selects a paper from the rack and reads it while having coffee."

"That sounds very sensible," she smiled, looking up from her breakfast plate. "I had a brief visit in Austria some time ago and I remember being served a delicious *sacher-torte* and coffee *mit schlag*."

The maid smiled. "Yes, Miss, coffee with whipped cream. Do you want some this morning?"

"No," she said. "Ordinary cream will do very nicely, thank you. And I see you have that on the tray."

"Yes, Miss."

"Have you worked here at this castle long?" Ina asked her.

"Yes," the woman nodded. "Nearly ten years. I was hired by the Madam when I first came to the village."

"Mrs. Leopold hired you?"

"Yes." The maid looked uneasy.

Ina asked her, "What do you make of her disappearance?"

The maid looked at her blankly.

Ina said, "Where do you think Madam has gone?"

The thin maid looked more distressed. "It is very bad. We do not talk about it. Madam was so good to everyone."

"What do you think happened to her?" Ina persisted.

"No one knows," the maid said in an awed voice.

"You must have some thoughts on the subject."

"There is evil in these mountains," the maid said. "Evil things which walk in the night!"

Ina knew the frightened woman was referring to ghosts, and this bore out what Claude had said, that the local people still had a lively vein of superstition. And it underlined Gretchen's suggestion that the ghost of Karl Bruck had come out of the past to whisk her mother off with him.

"Is there anything else, Miss?" the maid asked.

"Thank you, no," she said. She felt there was no point in questioning her further. She quite obviously didn't know anything, and putting a lot of questions to her only made her panicky.

She completed the excellent breakfast and felt better. Then she wrote a brief letter to her mother without mentioning any of the strange things she'd encountered. It was a pleasant, happy note meant to keep her parent from worrying. She hoped that it would. When she had addressed the envelope and sealed it, she started downstairs with it.

At the head of the stairs she was reminded of the events of the previous night. The whole terrifying episode came back to haunt her. She had a bad bruise on her elbow and also on the shoulder of the same arm. It seemed that she had landed on this arm when she toppled down the stairs. She could be thankful there was a heavy rug at the foot of the stairway which had helped soften her fall.

On the way down she heard the sound of Claude playing his violin from the music room. She had requested him to play for her but she hadn't expected to hear him so soon. It was a pleasing coincidence and she went directly to the music room to stand in the doorway and listen to him. His back was to her and so he did not see her but went on playing through the selection. When he finished she applauded.

Claude turned her way with a look of complete surprise. "I didn't know you were eavesdropping," he said.

"I enjoyed it very much," she told him.

He placed the violin in its case on the piano and put the

bow beside it. "I have to do some playing every day," he explained. "One soon loses skill otherwise."

"I can believe that," she said. "I hope I haven't made you stop playing sooner than you would have."

"Not at all," he said. "I had an early start. I won't do any more until later this afternoon."

She held up her letter. "I'd like to mail this."

"No problem," he said, taking it. "I'll see it is included with the outgoing mail." He gave her a concerned glance. "How do you feel this morning?"

"Better than I expected," she said.

"I'm glad."

"But I still remember last night very clearly," she told him.

He looked embarrassed. "Yes, last night. I'm giving all that some thought."

"I think you're just putting me off," she accused him.

"No," he protested. "Not at all. Just give me a little time and I'll come back to it."

They strolled from the music room together and reached the entrance hall. She halted and said, "I don't know what to do. I came here for an express purpose and now I can't go ahead with what I'd planned."

"Enjoy a holiday," Claude suggested. "That is what most people do who come here."

"I'm not your average tourist," she said.

"I know that. But seeing the tourist sights could fill in your time."

"I hardly feel like filling in time with Marta missing," she said. "I'd like to think I was doing something constructive about finding her."

"Leave that to father and me," Claude said.

"Have you contacted the police about that phone call?" she asked.

"I believe Father is looking after that," the young man said. "He made all the contacts with the police."

"Why?" she said, not fully satisfied.

He must have sensed her feelings for he quickly added, "It seems best to handle things that way. The police in these villages are not easy to deal with. And it makes it easier if one person looks after everything."

"I see," she said. "You mentioned talking to Hans about making another thorough search of the premises for Marta."

Claude showed embarrassment. "I'm waiting to speak to Hans. He went in to St. Anton to pick up some provisions this morning. I'll talk to him later."

She stared at him with worried eyes. "In other words, nothing is happening at all."

"Things are under way," he insisted.

"I'd say you were taking your time," was her reply.

As she finished speaking, Gretchen came part-way down the stairs and addressed them with her hand on the bannister. She said, "Someone was in my room when I was away." She had on a yellow negligee with a feather boa collar.

Claude stared up at her. "What do you mean?"

"One of my coats is missing," Gretchen said angrily. "That is what I mean. Someone has stolen my dark mink coat!"

Claude looked shocked. "When did you first notice it missing?"

"Just now," the blonde girl said. "And it must have happened the night of the New Year's Eve party. I wore the coat the day before."

David Leopold had appeared and was standing on the stairs with the blonde girl. The old man eyed her with annoyance. "What are you saying?"

"I'm telling you that one of your fine party guests must have walked off with my dark mink," she retorted angrily. "It must have been some party."

The gray-haired man gave her an exasperated look and then passed her on the stairs to come down and join Ina and Claude. He spoke to Claude: "You heard that?"

"Yes. I don't understand."

"I do," his father snapped. "That explains what Marta wore the night she vanished. She didn't go up to our room but she went to Gretchen's room, which is easier to get to, and took her fur coat. Wherever she is, you can be sure she's wearing that coat at this moment."

Ina listened with interest. It did seem to fit. Marta Landen had wanted to leave the house unnoticed and as quickly as she could. She didn't want to risk going to the room she shared with her husband so she went to Gretchen's room and got a fur coat there. Again it seemed clear it had been the phone call which had sent her out of the castle.

Gretchen called out angrily, "You're saying that Mother took my coat?"

"Who else?" David Leopold demanded.

"I suppose she could have," the blonde girl admitted in a less strident voice.

"Something else to tell the police," Claude said. And he asked his father, "Have you phoned the police yet?"

"No," David Leopold said testily. "I'm on my way to my study to attend to it now."

"Then you can also tell them about the missing coat," Claude said.

"You think I should?" his father worried. "I don't want to get them mixed up and thinking we're trying to find stolen property rather than a missing woman."

"I doubt if there'll be any risk of that," Claude said.

From the stairs Gretchen reminded them with exasperation, "I don't care what is said. I want my coat back." And she flounced up the stairs again to return to her room.

Claude gave Ina a resigned look. "You see what I told you? If you just wait, all the pieces will fall in place."

"I wonder," she said.

"And so do I," David Leopold chimed in, and then he walked away to make the phone call from his study.

Ina gave the young violinist a meaningful look. "If Marta took the fur coat, it begins to seem doubtful she is hiding in the castle."

"I told you we looked thoroughly."

"She must have had a phone call from someone she knew and agreed to meet him or her."

"I'd bet on it being a him."

"And?"

"It may be that I know who it was," Claude told her.

"How will you find out?"

He said, "I'll take you on a tour of the village and we'll stop by the ski lift and see how the jet set is represented."

She gave him a skeptical look. "You're sure you are serious about this? It's just not an excuse to drive me around?"

"I swear it," he said.

She went upstairs and put on a ski outfit she'd brought along which would be suitable for their excursion. It was dark with red trim and she had a red woollen cap to go with it. She completed her outfit with a red scarf which she wound around her neck. Then she went downstairs to join the young violinist.

Claude was waiting, also dressed in sports clothes. He gave her a smile of approval. "You look wonderful," he said.

"Thanks," she said. "What now?"

"I have my station wagon outside," he told her. "It's small but it has four-wheel drive and that can be handy in the snow."

They went out together and got into the tiny blue station wagon. As they drove along the road with its packed snow and high plowed snow on either side of it, Claude told her, "There are plenty of parties here just now. At this time of year *Fasching* parties are being held almost every night and there are ski races—part of the pre-Lenten revelry. And we wind up with a big party in costume called the *Faschingsdienstag,* which is our Austrian way of naming an Alpine Mardi Gras."

"It sounds exciting," she said.

At the wheel Claude nodded. "I loved them when I was a little boy. I used to watch from the landing as the guests arrived for the big party in their grotesque masks and costumes."

She glanced at him. "Then you used to have the big celebration at the castle?"

"One of them," he said. "There are dozens of parties

going on. Nearly all the hotels have one. But I don't see us continuing the tradition at the castle this year. Not without Mother. She was always the guiding spirit behind the affair."

"Perhaps she will come back before then."

His handsome face was grim as he watched the road. "I wish I could think that."

"Who are we going to see?" she asked him.

"You'll find out in good time."

"You enjoy being mysterious," she accused him.

"I value the effect of shock," he corrected her.

They drove into the quaint village and she again was delighted by the small houses with their elaborate gingerbread trim. They looked much like the ones seen in illustrations of the ancient fairy tales. The combination of colorful buildings set against the snow was irresistible. And then they left the village behind and drove toward the busy ski slopes.

Ina gasped as she saw there were literally hundreds of sports enthusiasts at different points on the slope. Claude parked the car by a combined restaurant and novelty shop and they made their way to a double-chair lift and waited their turn. Soon they were on the lift and being transported up the mountain side. Below the tops of tall evergreens reached up to her and she realized how far above the ground they were. The deep snow might make a good cushion to fall on, but if you were unlucky enough to strike a rock or become entangled in a tree any fall from the lift could be serious.

When they reached a high level they came to another ski shop. Standing amid a circle of a dozen skiers was a tall, good-looking man with very blonde hair. Ina at once spotted the man as a ski instructor.

Claude was giving her a grim smile. He said, "His name is Rolf Monner. And he could be the party we're looking for."

She glanced at Claude quickly. "You think he could be the one who phoned her New Year's Eve?"

"There's a good chance," Claude said, and catching the

ski instructor's eye he waved to him. Rolf Monner at once waved back. He continued to talk with the group of skiers around him for a few minutes longer and then he strode across to where Ina and Claude were standing.

He had good looks in a craggy Russian wolfhound manner. His face was narrow and long with high cheekbones and penetrating gray eyes. He nodded to Claude but he reserved his special attention for her.

"We haven't seen you up here in some time," he told Claude. "And now you come and bring a charming companion."

Ina had an idea she was supposed to melt under this compliment but she merely offered the tall ski instructor a thin smile.

Claude said, "May I introduce my cousin from America, Ina Sperling."

Rolf Monner bowed. "Delighted," he said. "I am Rolf Monner. I look after the skiers here and I'm always at your service."

"Thank you," she said. "You have a very impressive set-up."

"You are beginning to match our slopes in America," Rolf Monner said. "I spent some time in Denver last year and they've made great progress."

"In New England as well," she agreed.

"Are you an ardent skier?" the craggy-faced man wanted to know.

"A rank amateur," she said ruefully. "You'll have to assign me to your simplest slope."

"I regard that as a challenge," Monner assured her. "Stay long enough and I'll have you skiing like an expert."

"I doubt if I'll have that much time," she said.

Claude told the ski instructor, "Ina is a writer. She came here to help my mother with her memoirs."

Rolf showed a toothy smile. "And Marta should surely have plenty to tell. Where is she keeping herself? I haven't seen her lately either."

There was a moment's hesitation on Claude's part before he replied. He said, "When did you last see Mother?"

The ski instructor considered. "I believe it must have been before the New Year. Yes, I'm sure it was."

"You weren't in touch with her New Year's Eve, were you?" Claude asked.

Rolf Monner looked puzzled. "What do you mean?"

"You didn't phone her around the midnight hour by any chance?" Claude questioned him.

The tall man looked uneasy. "No," he said. But he was slow in getting his reply out.

"You're sure," Claude persisted.

The ski instructor seemed even more nervous as he said, "I'd remember if I had. It wasn't all that long ago. Why all the questions?"

Claude said, "My mother received a phone call from someone on New Year's Eve, just after the year had been rung in, and she vanished afterwards. None of us has seen or heard of her since."

Rolf Monner looked startled. He said, "You mean she's disappeared?"

"Yes," Claude said.

"She left no message? Nothing?"

Claude nodded. "That's the story."

The ski instructor gazed blankly from Claude to her. He said, "I don't understand it. It doesn't seem like Marta."

"I agree," Claude said. "I hoped you might be able to help."

"I know nothing about it," Rolf Monner said a little too hastily.

"Have you been talking with Gretchen?" Claude asked him.

"No. She and I had some trouble a while ago," he said evasively. "We don't see each other anymore."

"I see," Claude replied.

Rolf Monner said, "I have some people to see. If you'll both excuse me, I can't take any more time off at the moment." And with a nod to her, he added, "Nice meeting you, Ina. If you find the time, come see me. I'll get you started on the right slopes."

"Thank you," she said.

Claude watched after the tall, athletic man as he hurried over to the building which served as the center for the skiers at that level and went inside. There was a cynical look on the violinist's handsome face.

"He surely was in a hurry to get away," he said.

"I noticed that," she agreed.

Claude turned to her with a grim smile. "At least he made you an offer. He'd like to see you return on your own. Rolf has a way with attractive girls."

"I can see that he fancies himself."

"He's had the opportunity of proving himself a Casanova of the slopes for several years. His reputation is known in every ski center of the Alps."

She gave the young man a questioning look. "Do you think he was telling the truth when he said he didn't phone Marta on New Year's Eve?"

"I'm not sure."

"Just what was their relationship?"

"They were very friendly. Marta enjoyed the conquest of a younger man and he liked having his name linked with that of a movie star."

"You make them both sound like very shallow people."

"Rolf is a shallow person. Mother is a bit more complex but she has a weakness for tall, handsome men."

She frowned. "What did he mean about Gretchen being angry with him?"

Claude smiled bitterly. "Can't you guess?"

Her eyes widened. "You're saying Gretchen and Marta were rivals for Rolf's affection?"

"Gretchen saw him first. But she was bound to lose out when Marta discovered him and took an interest in him."

"What about your father?"

Claude shrugged. "My father loves Marta so much he is even willing to look the other way when she gets these crushes on other men."

"I'd say he was too tolerant."

"Perhaps. But he knows from experience such affairs never last long. Can you imagine Mother being seriously interested in a man like Rolf Monner for any length of time?"

"No."

"So you see?" Claude said. "All Father has to do in a case like this is be discreet and let time take care of the problem."

"Apparently Gretchen wasn't so willing to make way for Marta. She didn't want to lose Rolf."

"She didn't," Claude agreed. "And she and Mother had a serious row about him. I wasn't here at the time but I heard about it afterwards."

"A nasty situation," Ina said. "A mother and daughter in competition for the same man!"

"And a relatively worthless male at that," was Claude's grim reply. "It's not likely we'll get any more information from him now. We might as well go back down to the car."

It was easy to get back down on the cable car. Within a matter of a few minutes Claude was helping her into his car and they were driving back in the direction of the castle. The bright sunshine and the white snow everywhere lent a definite charm to the country setting. The evergreens with their mantle of snow added to the beauty as did the quaint buildings.

But not even the charm of the countryside could make her forget what their main purpose was. She turned to Claude at the wheel and asked, "Do you think he was really surprised when you told him about Marta having vanished?"

"If he wasn't he gave a good acting performance," was Claude's grim comment.

"I know," she agreed. "He did seem shocked. But there was still something in his manner which made me think he knows a lot more than he is willing to tell us."

"Of course you're right," Claude said. "And in spite of his denial it's still possible he made that phone call."

"What could he have said?"

"Asked Marta to meet him outside. He'd come by in his car and wait."

"And then?"

"Things might have gone badly. Rolf could have become enraged and attacked Mother. He could have killed her. That would mean his disposing of the body and denying having been in touch with her by phone or in person."

"You make it sound possible," she said, worried. "Do you think he's the killer type?"

"He could be if pushed far enough," was Claude's comment.

"How do you find out if he made the call?"

"I'll question around and see where he was New Year's Eve and who was with him."

"And?"

"Maybe I'll hit on some direct information about his party that night. It's not all that big a place. If I find out who he escorted I can perhaps discover if he made any phone calls around midnight."

"That would still only be conjecture," she worried. "Unless whoever was with him heard him mention Marta's name on the phone."

"That's most unlikely," Claude said.

"I'd say so."

"But it's worth a try to ask some questions in the proper places," Claude said. "For a start I could ask Gretchen if she saw him on that night. She was at a party at the hotel and didn't come home until next morning. She may be able to help us."

"If she will," Ina said.

"That's something else," Claude admitted. "She was pretty upset about her coat being missing."

"I noticed that."

"We may be doing this all wrong," the young violinist admitted. "But I don't know what else to do."

"You couldn't mention your suspicions of Rolf to the police?"

"No. They wouldn't get it at all."

"It gets no easier," she said as the castle loomed into sight against the snowy mountainside.

"I wonder if the call could have had anything to do

with Marta's proposed book," he said. "I've just remembered something."

"What?"

Claude kept his eyes on the snow-covered, narrow road as they neared the castle. "Rolf Monner is a German. His father was a Nazi and a kind of errand boy for Marta's friend, the notorious Karl Bruck. I've often heard Rolf laughing and boasting about what a good follower of Hitler his father was!"

She said, "You think he might have been worried that Marta would tell too much about his father in the book?"

"I'd say it was possible," Claude said, bringing the station wagon to a halt before the arched entrance door of the castle. "Wouldn't you?"

CHAPTER FIVE

Ina made no attempt to get out of the station wagon as she considered his question. She said, "It could well be Rolf wouldn't want his father written about. He may joke about the Nazi connection with intimates but it wouldn't help him in his job."

"Exactly," Claude said.

"Is his father still alive?"

"I don't know."

"It might be worthwhile to try and find out," she said. "That could make a difference."

"I'm not saying this theory is any good," Claude was quick to say. "But you have to go over everything in your mind."

"I know. Rolf Monner did behave a little strangely."

"But then the news about my mother was somewhat shocking. And since we know they were close it would be natural for him to be upset."

"True."

Claude looked at her with resignation. "So it is always a circle. We keep coming back where we started."

"I think something is gained every trip around," she said. "We get more information."

"For what it is worth."

She said, "Who can play the organ in the castle besides your mother?"

Claude stared at her. "Why do you ask that? We were talking about Rolf."

"I'm finished thinking about him," she said. "Now I'm back to last night. I didn't imagine all that, you know. I did hear the organ being played."

Claude sighed. "You might be better off to forget about it."

"I think not," she said. "Who else ever plays that organ?"

"I can play it," Claude admitted. "And Gretchen plays a little but not well."

She said, "Whoever I heard last night played expertly."

"Don't look at me!" he protested.

"You must admit you could be called the prime suspect."

"But you know better."

"Say I do," she said, "it could be that someone else who doesn't live in the house and who can play the organ wanted to throw some suspicion on you."

He furrowed his brow. "It's too fantastic! Who would want to play the organ at that hour of the night? And how could they manage it in any case? My father told you the organ was locked at the time you insisted you heard it being played."

"I even recognized the music," she said. "It was Wagner."

"That fits," Claude said grimly. "The Nazis loved his music."

"I thought of that," she agreed.

Claude sighed. "You'd better go in. I'll take the car around back and join you in a few minutes. I hope you don't think we wasted the morning."

"Not at all. It was interesting." And she left the car and went up the steps and into the castle.

When she entered the shadowed entrance foyer David Leopold and a large, middle-aged woman in a mannish black suit came to meet her. They had apparently been at the music room window and saw her arrive and enter the house.

David Leopold said, "May I introduce Miss Kate Bromley. For a number of years she was your aunt's personal secretary. She has been in England six months with her dying mother. Her mother passed away last week and Kate returned to resume her employment with Marta."

"I see," Ina said. And she turned to the woman, "How do you do, Miss Bromley. I am Marta's niece."

"Yes, she told me about you," Kate Bromley said rather stiffly. She was very British in accent and in looks. A gray-haired woman with a beefy face and the hulking, masculine figure which did not look well with skirts. Even the severe suit she was wearing did little for her.

David Leopold said, "Under the circumstances I don't know what to do. But the idea occurred to me that Miss Bromley might be of some assistance to you. She can tell you something about my wife's plans for the proposed book."

"That would be helpful," Ina agreed.

The lined face of the old man showed the tension he was under. "In the meanwhile we can only hope that Marta will return. You will excuse me, I'm weary. I'm going upstairs to rest. If you two want to talk, you are welcome to use the library."

"Thanks," Ina said. And she asked Kate Bromley, "Would you care to accompany me there?"

"All right," the British woman said.

Ina led the way, wondering just how intelligent Kate Bromley was and how much she knew about Marta Landen. One thing was fairly certain. The hefty Englishwoman secretary was devoted to her missing mistress.

The library always had a gloomy air about it. Ina went in first and took a chair near the desk and indicated a chair in which Kate Bromley could sit. "Do have a chair," she said.

"Thank you, Miss," the big woman said in the same stiff way as she sat gingerly in the chair, back straight and hands in her lap.

"Let's not stand on formalities," Ina said in her best reportorial manner. "I'm new to the house and things have been in a state since I reached here. I'll call you Kate and you may call me Ina."

"Call me Kate if you wish," the big woman said, studying her with grim eyes, "but I would prefer to call you Miss Sperling."

Ina sat back in her chair and waved a hand wearily. "Whatever you like then," she said. "You have been with Marta Landen for a long while?"

"Yes, Miss," the woman said. "I was first with her just after the Second World War. Though I'm British I had been living in Germany all during the war and I didn't want to go back to England. I only returned last year because of Mother being ill and alone."

Ina stared at her. "Do you mean you were a prisoner in Germany during the war?"

The big woman looked grim. "No, Miss. I was there by choice. I happen to be one of thse who believed in the Nazi regime. I went to Germany to train for political leadership in a British Nazi party. But the war came along and so I remained there."

"I see," said Ina, more than a little taken back. She was not sure that Kate Bromley would be anything but a hostile witness. She said, "You weren't with Marta Landen during the war though?"

"No. I saw her in films and on the stage. I was a fan of hers," the big woman said. "But I had not met her."

"That came about after the war?"

"Yes," Kate Bromley said. "I was looking for a job and I learned that Miss Landen wanted a secretary who was proficient in English. I applied for the job and was hired."

"You came directly here?"

"Yes."

"Was Marta married to David Leopold then?"

"Yes," Kate said. "But they'd only been married a few months. He was a wreck of a man then. Not anything like he is now. He regained his health in a marvelous manner."

"So I gather."

"And she had adopted Mr. Claude. He was just a boy. A

fine lad, though he was sickly and thin then. But he grew up into a credit to Miss Marta."

"I agree," Ina said dryly. "Did Marta know about your Nazi affiliation?"

The big woman's face turned crimson. "I could hardly hide it from her. Nor did I try to."

Ina raised her eyebrows. "And she wasn't upset? I mean, she had just married a Jewish survivor of a concentration camp and adopted a Jewish boy. Why would she want you, an admitted ex-Nazi, in her house?"

Kate Bromley looked belligerent. "I believed in most of Hitler's ideas," she said, "but I did not approve of his treatment of the Jews. I did not know anything about the concentration camps or what had gone on in them until after the war. I was sickened and so were many others like me."

Ina stared at her. "You're telling me you lived in Germany during those years and worked for the party and didn't know what was going on?"

Once again the big woman's face crimsoned. She said, "I knew that the Nazi government did not trust Jews in responsible posts because of a Communist plot against us. I realized restrictions had been placed on them and many had been placed in protective arrest."

"The concentration camps with their gas chambers and furnaces were hardly prisons for protective arrest."

Kate Bromley's lips were compressed firmly. "I have never believed all of those stories," she said.

"I know them to be true. I saw the newsreels and I have read the authenticated documents pertaining to them," Ina told her.

"Newsreels and photographs can be faked," Kate declared. "And everyone tells a different story. I knew nothing of what was happening in those camps. And I suspect the Führer didn't either. He was a good man."

"As you say, everyone tells a different story," was Ina's grim reply.

"I survived the atrocity bombings by the British and Americans," Kate declared. "I was in Hamburg and I know. But I have never held hatred in my heart. And I have never been a bigot. I did not have any bad feelings toward the Jews and Miss Landen accepted that."

Ina listened with a good deal of disbelief. She had heard that many Germans told the same story that Kate had repeated for her just now. But she was inclined to think it pure fiction. Marta Landen had herself been a Nazi sympathizer. When it became propitious she had married a Jew and adopted a Jewish child. But Ina felt sure that this was only a gesture to the changing times. If Marta were still alive she probably held strong loyalty to the Nazis who had been her friends in the old days. Even the castle had likely been given to her by Karl Bruck. Marta had probably hired Kate because she secretly sympathized with her.

Ina said quietly, "I'll accept your explanation, Kate, though I must say it is difficult for me to understand. And of course you know that Marta has disappeared?"

"Yes. Isn't it awful! I should never have left her!" Kate lamented.

This interested her. She said, "You think if you'd been here this wouldn't have happened?"

The big woman looked uneasy. "I didn't exactly mean that. But I was close to Miss Marta and kept a sharp eye on her. She wouldn't have gotten out of the house without my knowing it."

"Her husband thinks she may have suffered an attack of amnesia and wandered out into the night."

"He told me," Kate Bromley said. "But I don't think that is what happened."

"Why?"

"Miss Marta was never ill. She had nothing wrong with her mind. She was as healthy as any of us. Oh, she became lonesome and depressed when she wasn't working, but nothing more."

"So you don't believe she's lost her memory?"

"No. I think it must have been something else."

"What?"

"I couldn't say that, Miss," the big woman hedged. "I'm

not one of the family. I'm hired help. It is not for the likes of me to make statements."

Ina said, "I hope you're not going to start hinting about ghosts and that kind of thing. I've heard enough about the phantom of Karl Bruck being seen on the slopes and in this house."

Kate Bromley looked indignant. "Those that say that are fools! People who hated Karl Bruck and Miss Marta! They know that he once was a guest here and they try to use it to hurt Miss Marta's good name!"

"That wouldn't surprise me," Ina agreed. "You don't have to be afraid to talk frankly to me. I am Marta's niece by marriage. My uncle was drowned in the stream on the estate."

"I've heard that talked about. Miss Marta was very sad until she married Mr. David."

"So I understand," she said. "Now have you any thoughts about Marta vanishing? Please don't be afraid to be frank."

The big woman hesitated. Then she said, "I shouldn't say it, but Miss Gretchen gave her a lot of trouble."

"You think the bad feeling between Gretchen and her mother might account for Marta's vanishing?"

"I think so. There was a man—a ski instructor."

"Rolf Monner?"

"I think that was his name."

"You knew of the rivalry between them for that young man?"

Kate Bromley looked unhappy. 'It was impossible not to know. They had many quarrels, and some of them loud enough to be heard all through the building."

"I see," she said. "Is that all you have to suggest?"

"Yes," Kate Bromley said. "I think you should question Miss Gretchen."

"I'm sure she has been questioned," Ina said. "And no doubt she will be again. There is one other thing. You know I came here chiefly to work on my aunt's biography."

"Yes."

"Did she ever discuss this with you?"

"Many times."

"What did she say?"

Kate Bromley said, "I typed out a number of stories as she recalled them. She wanted them ready when she began work on the book. I began two years ago before that young man came here to help her."

Ina recalled a brief mention of someone who had worked with her aunt before. "What about him?" she asked. "A journalist from Berlin. His name was Conrad something or other. He began putting the various items together. He lived here in the house and worked every afternoon with Miss Marta until she went to Italy to make a film. He remained behind to type out the opening portions of the book for her to read on her return."

"Go on," Ina said.

The big Englishwoman said, "It's an old story, Miss Sperling. That young man was here with Miss Gretchen and she can be hard to resist. By the time her mother came back here the two were carrying on a romance. Miss Marta didn't approve of that at all. She ordered the young man out of the house and gave up the idea of the book. Not until she got in touch with you did she revive it again."

"What about her original notes and the work done by that young man?" she asked.

"Miss Marta put all the material away somewhere. I have no idea what she did with it. But just before I left for England she told me she had a niece in New York who was a professional writer and she had decided to write her and see if she would help with the book. Miss Marta felt it was the proper moment to have it published. I guess that is when she got in touch with you."

"Yes, I would say so. And you have no idea where the notes for the book are?"

"No, Miss Sperling."

"If Miss Marta doesn't return and I decide to do the book anyway I will need those notes badly. They must be found."

Kate Bromley looked distressed. "But Miss Marta will return. She must!"

"I sincerely hope so," she said. "But we can't be sure until we hear from her or see her again."

"It's a dreadful thing!" the woman lamented.

"It is."

"Do you want me for anything else?" Kate Bromley asked.

"No. Not at the moment. And thank you for being so cooperative," Ina said. "It was considerate of you." She was on her feet now.

The big woman had also risen and was staring down at her heavy black oxfords, avoiding Ina's eyes. She said, "I'm pleased to have been of some help."

"You have been a big help, believe that," Ina assured her.

"If I may, Miss, I'll go to my room now," the woman said.

"Of course. And don't forget to bring me the material for the book if you happen to come across it."

"I promise that I will," Kate Bromley said and then she turned and marched out of the room.

Ina watched her go with some mystification. In addition to being a huge, ungainly creature, she had a complexity of personality which was quite astonishing. Ina was sure the woman was clever and was covering up a good deal for her mistress. Perhaps as Ina got to know Kate better she would learn more.

Going out into the corridor she met Claude. He said, "I've been looking for you."

"I was in the library with Kate Bromley."

The young violinist looked none too pleased. "Is she back? I had hoped she would have stayed in England. That woman had a diabolical hold over Marta."

"How?"

"I have no idea but I know it to be true," he told her.

"Did your mother never resent her?"

He frowned. "She simply refused to talk about her."

"That doesn't surprise me," Ina said. "The woman is a mass of contradictions."

"Kate doesn't see herself that way," Claude warned her.

"I know," she said. "What surprised me most is that she is an unashamed Nazi sympathizer."

"She told you then? I wondered. I was going to mention it."

"She spoke about her membership in the party right away. She appeared to be rather proud of it."

"If you can imagine such a thing," Claude agreed. "Yet in spite of everything she was good to me as a child. I won't forget that. I was with her a lot when Mother was away doing a film or play. Kate was good to me."

"I can believe that," Ina said. "She's simply confused in a political sense. As a person she's fairly sound. She has some thoughts about your mother's disappearance."

"Tell me," he said, his handsome face showing interest.

"It seems all routes lead to Rolf Monner."

"She mentioned him?"

"And the trouble between your mother and Gretchen as they quarreled about him."

"Anything else?"

"She suggested I question Gretchen, which I will do."

"Gretchen has been questioned," Claude reminded her. "I don't think she knows anything more than she's told us. But I do believe we've got to concentrate on Monner now. And Gretchen may be able to help there."

She gave him a wise look. "You'll want to do that questioning on your own."

"Probably," he agreed.

She stood there in the shadowed hallway with him feeling a new uneasiness. A sense of not being able to fully trust him. And so she said, "There is something else."

"What?"

"Marta had a young man here working on her book a couple of years ago. Someone from Berlin."

Claude showed surprise. "Yes, she did. Conrad Ritter. Didn't you know about him?"

"Your mother mentioned a young man briefly in her letter. But she didn't give any details. And no one else said anything until Kate mentioned him."

"I guess no one felt it was important."

"It seems to me it has importance," she said. "At least for me. There were notes dictated by Marta and a lot of other material he compiled. I don't know what has happened to it."

Claude said, "Nor do I. You know what happened, don't you?"

"According to Kate a romance sprang up between this young man and Gretchen while her mother was away. Marta was angry when she came back and discovered the affair and ordered this Conrad out of the house."

"I wasn't at home then," Claude said. "But that's the way I heard it so I'd say it was true."

Ina smiled grimly. "So it seems I was second choice."

"I'm sure Mother was more excited at the prospect of working with you," he said. "It was merely that she'd never thought of you before."

"I might have been lucky if she hadn't thought of me at all."

The handsome young man gave her a reproving look. "Then we might never have met."

"I hadn't thought about that," she said.

"Please do," he said in a quiet voice. Then he asked her, "Have you seen Father?"

"Yes. He was here when I first came in. He introduced Kate to me. Then he left us and went upstairs. He complained of not feeling too well."

"Mother's disappearance has hit him hard," Claude said in a worried voice. "You have no idea how devoted those two are to each other."

She gave him a wise glance. "Didn't Marta have an odd way of showing it?"

Claude's face flushed. "She couldn't help an occasional affair but it meant nothing. It is Father she really loves. And he knows it."

"I won't pretend to understand," she said. "But from all I hear Marta couldn't have been an easy person to live with or to like.

"I've never pretended she was. But she still has a lot to offer."

"I hope I may meet her and judge, if she's still alive," she said. "I'd think that every day that passes without her returning makes it more likely she's dead."

"You're probably right."

"What about the police?"

"That's why I want to talk to Father," Claude said. "He was to get in touch with them. I want to hear the latest report."

"You've given up the idea of another search of the castle?"

"There's the coat she took from Gretchen. I don't think she'd have gone to the trouble to get that if she'd been going to remain in the house."

"So right now you're assuming she had a call from Rolf Monner and went out to join him in his car?"

"Yes," he said. "After that I have no idea what happened. But I'm going to try and find out."

They went upstairs together with Claude leaving her at the first landing to go and see his father. She went on up to the third floor. She was still trying to digest all that she'd learned from her interview with Kate Bromley. And she was ready to admit that there were many things about life in the castle which she did not understand and might never understand!

Her mother had never liked Marta. And very gradually she was coming around to the same point of view. From all the evidence she had gathered, Marta was a devious woman who used other people like pawns to get what she wanted. Her latest move had been to decide to publish a frank and startling book of memoirs to bring her notoriety and work again. She would not care whom she hurt in doing it. And very likely someone resenting the project had determined to eliminate her.

That was Ina's feeling about the matter. She also felt almost certain that wherever Marta might be she was dead by now. The other theory which Claude was clinging to, in which Rolf Monner played a major role, did not seem logical to her. But she was perfectly willing to allow the young violinist to pursue it to a conclusion.

What amazed her was that most of these people felt Marta had a good side despite the many wicked and cruel things she had done. It was a tribute to the personality of the actress that this should be true. People, including those close to her like David and Claude and even Kate Bromley, allowed themselves to be blinded by her false glamour. Only Gretchen expressed disgust and hatred for her mother. Perhaps, being so much like her, she understood her better than the others.

Ina had misgivings about remaining in St. Anton and particularly about remaining at the castle. It seemed inevitable if she stayed that she should get more deeply involved in Marta's affairs. And knowing what she did now, it wouldn't be a pleasant experience. No doubt the book which could come out of it would be sensational, but Ina had no stomach for scandalous journalism.

She knew she had heard the organ being played the previous night and she suspected that it might have been Marta or her ghost at the keyboard. Then she had encountered that other phantom creature with the horribly disfigured face. None of the others had paid any attention to her claims, suggesting she'd been the victim of a bad nightmare. But she knew this simply wasn't so.

What could she expect next? A confrontation with the phantom figure of the long-dead Nazi Karl Bruck? A lot of people thought his evil spirit still ruled the castle. And perhaps it did. The evil which men leave after them was known to be a potent force. In view of everything, she would be perhaps well advised to pack her bags and take the express train back to Paris.

She opened the door of her room and went in. As she entered she gasped. For there was Gretchen standing by the window staring out at the snow-capped mountains. The blonde girl turned with a mocking smile on her pretty but somewhat haggard face.

Gretchen said, "Are you angry at me for being here?"

"I hadn't thought about that. I was merely startled."

"I wanted to talk to someone. I thought you were up here. But the room was empty. So I waited."

"That I see."

"Where were you?"

Ina was wary. "Claude took me for a drive. We went to the village and then as far as the slopes."

Gretchen inclined her head to one side, so her long golden hair draped on her shoulder. "Ah, the slopes!"

"Yes."

"Of course you met Rolf Monner?"

She felt there was no point in denying it. "Yes," she said, "I did."

"How did you like him?"

Ina shrugged. "I didn't get too definite an impression of him. He's good-looking and virile. I would expect him to be extremely popular."

Gretchen smiled rather bitterly. "I'm surprised you aren't more ecstatic. Most females find him irresistible."

"Oh?"

"I did."

"Well, now I know. I must watch him more closely in the future."

"You'll see him again if you interested him," Gretchen said. "With me it was no good. Mother entered the picture and spoiled it all. We battled about him and I let her have him. It was really a dreadful display on our parts. I shudder now when I think about it."

"I'm sorry," she said.

"About Rolf and me? No need to be," Gretchen said carelessly "He's really no good, you know. He'd have broken my heart in the end. But I just didn't like to lose him to Mother."

"I understand," she said.

Gretchen shook her head. "You say so but I doubt if you do. All my life I've been like Mother's tiny shadow. A shadow which she's resented, tried to lose, and make miserable. But there is this odd thing about a shadow; it imitates you, tries to flatter you that way, and you never escape it no matter how hard you try."

Ina was embarrassed by this frank talk. She said, "I can guess it isn't easy to be the daughter of a celebrity."

"And Mother never forgot for a moment she was a celebrity," Gretchen said with a sigh. "But now that she's no longer here for me to quarrel with, I'm lost. After all, what is a shadow without the real person? It ceases to exist."

"Everyone seems to think your mother will come back."

"I don't," Gretchen said.

"Really?"

"I'm almost sure she's dead. I wasn't merely talking wildly when I said the ghost of Karl Bruck must have reached out from the past for her. I think that is what happened in a way. This castle is still haunted by him."

"You honestly feel that?"

"I do," Gretchen said. "And as soon as I can I'm going to get away from here. If Mother doesn't return perhaps I'll be able to try acting again. Without her to interfere I might even succeed."

"Why do you connect her disappearance with the ghost?"

"You should know," Gretchen said, looking at her very directly. "This old castle has been the scene of many weird happenings. I've always felt there was something strange about the way my father met his death. Mother would never talk about it and that made me even more suspicious."

"He did die suddenly," Ina agreed.

"And then there was Conrad," the other girl said.

"You mean the young man who came here a while ago to write the book with your mother," she said. "I understood she sent him away."

"So she did," Gretchen agreed. "But that was only part of it. I tried to reach him afterwards and couldn't."

"Why not?"

The blonde girl gave her a meaningful look. "Because he had vanished. He was supposed to go back to Berlin. But to the best of my knowledge he never got there. He simply dropped out of sight and I've never heard of him again."

The news was startling. She stared at the girl. "You're

saying that this young man vanished in almost the identical way your mother did?"

"Yes."

"And he had been going to collaborate with her in writing her memoirs just as I came here prepared to do?"

"That's right," Gretchen said. "It seems there must be a kind of curse on anyone who tries to delve into my mother's past. So you'd better be careful!"

"It begins to sound like good advice," Ina said wryly. "Claude thinks I should try to do the book on my own if Marta doesn't return."

"Claude isn't aware of the danger," the blonde girl warned her. "He spends most of his time touring the concert circuits. He's lost in his own world."

"David Leopold should understand the situation," she said.

Gretchen looked scornful. "My stepfather is only a shell of a man. He puts on a good front but there is little behind it. He is content to sit here in the castle and pore over his rare books and his stamp collection. He's still frightened by what he went through in the concentration camps. All he wants is to be left alone. That is why he allowed my mother to behave as she liked. His spirit is shattered."

"I hadn't thought of him in that light," Ina admitted.

"Look more closely next time," was her blonde cousin's advice.

"What about Kate Bromley?"

Gretchen laughed with sour humor. "That left-over Nazi? She's a pitiful example of what happens to some women when they endorse causes. Hers turned out to be a despicable one and she still won't admit it."

"I'm sure she's very devoted to your mother," Ina said.

"Perhaps," Gretchen said. "I wouldn't really know because I don't think you can easily read the minds of people like her. But she does seem dedicated to the Marta Landen cult. But then my mother was once the darling of the Nazis. Don't forget that."

"It would be hard to overlook her association with them in writing about her," Ina said.

Gretchen's pretty face was clouded. "I think all that evil has returned in some odd fashion. Perhaps brought back because my mother was going to expose some of the evil secrets of those bad days. And in the end it just overwhelmed her."

Ina was standing close to the blonde girl. She said, "I don't find your reasoning easy to follow."

Gretchen gave her a strange look. "I don't expect you to. But I will give you a word of advice. Leave here! You've been close to the book material and you could be next to suffer. I'd get away from here as soon as I could rather than wait for something to happen."

"What could happen?"

Gretchen shrugged. "We might wake up one morning to find you had also vanished."

"I hardly think so!"

"Don't be too sure about anything!"

Ina sighed. "Your stepfather wants me to remain here."

"Perhaps to make him feel easier," was Gretchen's reply. "Can you imagine how he must panic inside? He's the least able to fight the mystical curse of those long-dead Nazis. They crushed him to a pulp then—what do you think they might do to him now?"

"I'm not afraid of ghosts," Ina said. "Not even those of the Nazi variety."

Gretchen eyed her sorrowfully. "Well, when the time comes just remember I warned you."

Even in the sunshine of the big bedroom the blonde girl's words had a sinister ring to them. Ina listened to her with a fear that she knew a great deal more than she was going to reveal. It was the same with the others in the castle. They all gave the impression of being involved in some evil larger than themselves.

She said, "I'm going to stay a few more days in the hope your mother will return."

"And then?"

"I don't exactly know," she said. "If she continues to be

missing I'll either have to go back to New York or see what I can dig up here and try to whip a book in shape anyway."

Gretchen stared at her. "I'd call that foolhardy."

"Even though Claude and his father approve of it?"

"You should pay no attention to them," the other girl said scornfully.

Ina studied Gretchen's pale face. "You're very different from what I expected. I have no other cousins and I looked forward to this meeting."

Gretchen went across to the door and turned the knob as if to leave, but she hesitated to tell Ina over her shoulder, "Well, now we've met. Be smart. Make sure you live to remember it." And with that puzzling comment she went on out, closing the door after her.

CHAPTER SIX

That evening there were guests for dinner. When Ina went down to join the others for the evening meal she found the two strangers there with the others. David Leopold came forward with an uneasy smile on his lined face and introduced her to the visiting couple.

"Ina, I want you to meet our neighbors, Pauline and Otto Fess," the gray-haired man said. "They are long-time friends of Marta and I'm sure they are interested in meeting her niece from America."

Otto Fess stepped up to her first and bowed in a stiff old-fashioned way. "A great pleasure, Miss Sperling," he said in a heavily-accented voice. He was a thin, gaunt man in his sixties. His grizzled gray hair was thin at the temples and he had a deep scar on his left cheek which ran from just below the eye to the chin line. It could have been an old dueling scar.

She said, "You live near here?"

"We have the adjoining property," Otto Fess said in his halting English. "We came here about the same time your aunt took over this place. So Marta became our close friend."

Ina asked, "Did you know my uncle, Ralph Sperling?"

Fess nodded. "We were here when he drowned. It was shocking. You see my wife, Pauline, was also an actress and she appeared with Marta in one of your uncle's plays."

Pauline Fess smiled for Ina's benefit and she became

aware of the strange burning eyes in the wrinkled, brown face of the elderly woman. In almost perfect English in contrast to her husband's heavy efforts, she said, "You are here to write the book!"

"I'm no longer certain," she said, "because of what happened to Marta."

"But you mustn't give up now," the thin, faded woman said. Her black hair was obviously dyed, and she wore a print dress which was badly out of style. "I was to be in the book. Marta promised me! You must write it and put me in it!"

Her husband turned to the woman with a look of annoyance. "Miss Sperling must do what she thinks best. I can certainly understand her not wanting to go ahead with anything until we know what has become of Marta."

Pauline Fess gave her husband a look of reproach. "But I already know about Marta! She is dead! I saw her ghost last night!"

The old woman's plaintive words brought a moment of tense silence to the drawing room. Ina was shocked and saw looks of fear and apprehension on the faces of most of the others. The unhappy silence was broken by Otto Fess laughing harshly.

The gaunt man said, "You and your notions, my dear! You think you are still on the stage! Always acting and pretending mad things!" And he moved her away from Ina.

Ina was watching after her when Claude came up by her side and in a low voice said, "Don't pay any attention to her."

She gave him a baffled look. "What did she mean?"

"Nothing! Pauline Fess is mad. She has been for some time. It is getting worse. She has hardening of the arteries. It's sad. Once she was quite a beauty and a very good actress. At least that's what my mother claimed."

"So that's it," she said.

Claude continued talking in a quiet voice as he guided her toward the dining room with the others, "Mother used to have them come over here regularly. She felt sorry for

Pauline and poor old Otto. We pay no attention to what she says and pretend everything is normal."

"I'm glad you told me," she said.

"I tried to get to you before Father introduced them," the young man said. "But I didn't have time."

They joined the rest of the party in the wood-paneled dining room and Hans served a fine meal. Ina was far enough away from Pauline so that she was not bothered by the old woman. She could see David Leopold carrying on a conversation with her and noticed that he seemed to be under a strain.

After dinner the party gathered in the drawing room again and Claude played several selections for them. Ina listened to the young violinist with rapt attention, impressed by his talent. Then there was general conversation again and Ina was unfortunate enough to be singled out by the ailing Pauline.

The thin woman's burning eyes fixed on her and she smiled at her and asked, "Have I met you?"

"Earlier," Ina said politely. "I'm Marta Landen's niece."

Pauline Fess nodded. "Of course. It was stupid of me not to remember. My memory fails me often these days."

"You have lived here a long while?"

The elderly woman nodded. "We came here directly after my husband was discharged from the army. Before that he had been in business. But the war ruined the business and so he decided to retire and live here."

Ina said, "And you were on the stage?"

"Yes," the old woman agreed. "I was an actress. I appeared with Marta many times. Karl Bruck had me meet her. He was a dear friend of my husband."

"Was he?"

"Oh, yes," Pauline Fess went on, "it was Karl who brought us up here and showed us the mountains. He had already bought this place for Marta. He planned to come here and live. But then the collapse came and he did not survive it."

Ina was listening with growing interest. The aging actress had confirmed the rumor that the castle had been owned by Bruck, who'd turned it over to Marta. She wondered how much more the actress knew about those early days and how reliable her comments might be.

Ina asked her, "What was the last time you saw Karl Bruck?"

The thin woman leaned close to her and in a confidential tone said, "You must keep it a secret. But I saw him only last night!"

"Last night?"

Pauline Fess nodded, her eyes as strangely bright as ever. "I was standing by the window of my room staring out at the snowy hills with the moonlight on them. Don't you enjoy moonlight winter nights?"

"Yes," she said impatiently, "but you were telling me about Karl Bruck."

"Dear Karl!" the old woman said, and then looked lost. She gave her a troubled glance. "What was I saying about him?"

"You said you had seen him last night but you didn't explain yourself."

Pauline Fess glanced over her shoulder to make sure no one was overhearing them and then she said in a conspiratorial tone, "I saw him suddenly come down the slope at a tremendous speed."

"Karl Bruck?"

"Yes. He was on skis and wearing his uniform just as he had when we last met. He looked so stalwart, so soldierly coming down on his skis in his officer's uniform."

"Are you sure you saw him?" Ina asked her.

The old woman looked annoyed. "Why do people always question me so? Of course I saw him. His ghost comes down that hill on skis almost every moonlit night."

"His ghost?"

"Yes," the old woman said irritably. "I have the power to see spirits, you know. I see Karl's regularly. And now I'm seeing Marta's. She comes to me in the night looking young and lovely as she did when she was a girl and Karl was in love with her. What a fine pair they made!"

Ina tried to placate the excited old woman. "Don't you

think you must dream some of those things or maybe even imagine them? You can't have seen Marta's ghost since she's probably not dead."

Pauline Fess became angry. "I know who I saw! It was Marta! She smiled at me and told me I'd been very good in the play.

It was sadly apparent that the old woman was rambling, mixing up what had happened years before with the present. It would be silly to pay any attention to what she had to say.

Ina told her, "I'm sure you have many happy memories."

"I live surrounded by phantoms," the old woman said brightly. "They tell me their secrets."

"That must be very interesting for you," Ina said, humoring the madwoman as she searched the group for someone to rescue her. But all the others were in conversation or had their backs to her.

"Do you do needlework?" Pauline Fess wanted to know.

"No."

"What a pity! I do! And so did Marta! Before she died she left her needlework basket with me!"

Ina gave the old woman a vexed look. "Why do you keep saying Marta is dead? We don't know that. She's probably as much alive as we are."

"No," the old woman said slyly, "you don't confuse me that way. I know what I know!"

Ina was about to try and reason with the old woman again when suddenly her husband approached with a worried expression on his gaunt face. The scar on his cheek seemed more livid than when she'd first noticed it.

"What are you doing, my dear?" he demanded of his wife in a harsh voice. "I hope you're not bothering this young lady."

"No, Otto," the thin woman said tremulously. "We were just talking about the old days."

"I'm sure Miss Sperling has no interest in your recollections of the old days," her husband said in exasperation. He gave Ina an apologetic look. "You mustn't mind my wife!"

"We had a nice conversation," she said politely.

Pauline Fess smiled. "You see? I have done no harm. I have only told her about the ghosts. Of how I see Karl come down the slope on his skies. What a noble figure he makes in the moonlight!"

Otto Fess took his wife angrily by the arm. "That is enough," he said. And he bowed to Ina. "You will please excuse us." Then he dragged his wife away to say good night to David Leopold and Gretchen. After that they immediately left.

Claude came over to where Ina was standing by the fireplace. He said, "I saw Pauline Fess tackling you again."

"Yes. I was in a panic. She talked very well at first and then began saying a lot of wild things. I couldn't get away from her."

"I was talking to her husband. As soon as I saw what was going on, I drew his attention to her and he went over."

She smiled ruefully. "So I owe my rescue to you."

"I don't deserve much credit," the curly-haired young man said. "I ought to have noticed sooner."

"Just so long as I was rescued. She really can go on a lot of wild nonsense."

"Her mind wanders."

"She was full of seeing Karl Bruck coming down the slopes on skis. And for an added touch she saw him in full uniform!"

He shook his head. "I suppose she knew Bruck in the old days."

"She said she did. And she's convinced your mother is dead."

The young man's handsome face was grave. "I know. I heard her saying that. It made cold shivers run down my spine."

"She was only fantasizing," Ina said.

"It makes you wonder," he said gloomily. "The mad are said to have a kind of second sight. It would be strange if she were right. The longer we go on without word from my mother, the more uneasy I'm becoming."

"Gretchen seems certain her mother is dead."

Claude looked angry. "You mean that's what she wants."

"It's what she says. She's very bitter about Marta. She went over the whole story about Rolf Monner. I think she felt very badly about that."

"I'm sure she did. But it was best for her. Rolf is a rotter," the young man said.

"I think you're right, but it was still a hard blow to have her mother be the one to steal him from her. I'd say Gretchen is very tired of being dominated by her mother."

"We'll see what happens now that Mother is no longer here," he said.

"There's something else."

"What?"

"About that fellow who came to work on Marta's book."

"Conrad?"

"Yes. According to Gretchen, she tried to contact him at his Berlin address after he left here but she couldn't reach him. He seemed to have vanished in thin air."

Claude looked at her incredulously. "Gretchen told you that?"

"Yes."

"It's the first I've heard of it," he said. "Of course I was away at the time. Why don't you ask Father about it?"

"I will," she said.

"He should be able to tell you all the facts."

"He's probably gone to his study after seeing the Fesses out," she said. "I'll try him there."

"Could you let it wait until morning?"

"No. I'll see if he's still at his desk. Otherwise I'll wait."

Claude and she walked out to the hallway and he said good night and went upstairs. She had intended to compliment him on his playing but he got away before she had a chance. She blamed herself for getting too wrought up about the various mysteries she'd encountered in the old castle. And she promised herself that she'd mention the short violin recital to him as soon as they met in the morning.

Reaching the door of the study she saw that Kate Bromley was standing before David Leopold's desk. The big woman was talking to him in German in a low voice. He replied to her in the same language at a rapid rate. Ina heard the exchange without being able to understand what was being said.

After a moment Kate Bromley came marching out of the room. She saw Ina standing by the doorway and glared at her. Then she went on without saying a word.

Ina went into the study and walked over to David Leopold's desk. "I'm sorry," she said, "I didn't mean to interrupt anything."

"You didn't, he said with a sigh. "Miss Bromley was here complaining that she wasn't given the same room she had before. It is just as good a room but she is enraged because she was moved. She can be a very unreasonable woman!"

"I thought she was in a rage about something," Ina said. "She went by me like a thundercloud."

"You must not mind her," David Leopold said. "She is very odd and dedicated to Marta. With my wife missing she feels lost here. It is very difficult."

Ina asked him, "Have you heard any further word from the police?"

"Nothing of any importance. They are continuing to search for Marta."

It struck her that he was accepting the situation without much concern. Or at least he didn't seem as troubled as he had when she'd first arrived. And she began to wonder if Marta might not have gone too far in betraying her husband. David Leopold might no longer care whether she was alive or dead. He must surely suspect that the New Year's Eve call had come from Rolf Monner and that she'd gone to meet him. But he was taking it quite calmly.

She also realized what a disadvantage she had in not being able to speak German. It stopped her from making any real investigation on her own.

She said, "The police don't seem to be having much luck, do they?"

Leopold looked up at her wearily. "You know how it is. I'm sure they're not devoting their full time to searching for Marta. They have many other problems."

"Of course."

He stared at the top of his desk. "I had to be careful in presenting the problem to them," he explained. "We don't want any scandal. And Marta could be with some other man. I guess you know that. You've heard enough about her by now to be familiar with her weakness."

"It is too bad," she said. "Marta could be in real trouble or already the victim of some murderer."

"I think not," the gray-haired man said, glancing wearily up at her again. "No, I think not."

From his manner she began to suspect he had some idea of where Marta was and with whom she might be. What surprised her was that he seemed to have lost his confidence that she would return.

She asked him, "Had either of the Fesses anything to offer?"

"No. They haven't seen her since before New Year's. They're not too active these days. He is not in good health and you are aware of his wife's mental state."

"Yes."

"Marta was kind to them because of the old days," he went on. "I didn't know them as well as she did. But it seems I should go on entertaining them since they were her friends."

She said, "They also were friends of Karl Bruck."

"No doubt," Leopold sighed. "As you may know, Otto Fess was in the army. In the latter days of the war the Führer called on men of all ages. And even though Otto was really past military service age, he answered the call of his country. He and I have little in common beyond the present. I never discuss those other times with him."

"Perhaps it is best," she said.

David Leopold gave her a grim look. "I have a very special feeling of hatred toward Karl Bruck. I'm sure you can understand that. His memory poisons this house and perhaps poisoned my marriage to Marta as well."

"He must have been a very evil man," she said.

"He was," Marta's husband said quietly.

"I came in to ask you about that young man who was here for a time working on the book with Marta."

"What about him?"

"I know that he didn't work out," she said. "And that he was sent away. But I have heard that after he left here he simply vanished."

"Who told you that?" David Leopold asked sharply.

She hesitated, then said, "Gretchen."

The elderly man rose from behind his desk and came around to stand by her. He said solemnly, "I'm sure you can guess why she told you such a story."

"Not really."

His eyes were sad. "She and her mother were quarreling about Conrad as they've quarreled over so many other men. A disgraceful business!"

"She admitted that," Ina said. "But she insisted that she never could reach him again."

"Then she was lying to you," David Leopold said. "I had a letter from him with a demand for extra money for the work he did here. And when he didn't get a reply from me, I heard from his lawyer."

"So he did turn up in Berlin?"

"He most surely did," the old man said. "I refused to pay him any more because he hadn't fulfilled his contract. The matter was dropped and since then I have not had any communication with him. But I have no doubt he is still in Berlin."

"Thank you for explaining," she said. "I wondered."

"Do you think you will try the book alone if Marta does not come back?" David Leopold asked.

"Perhaps. It depends on how much material turns up. Kate Bromley claims she typed quite a lot of dictated matter. But she has no idea where it is now."

"I wouldn't be surprised if that other young writer

hadn't stolen it and taken it with him," Marta's husband declared.

"You think there's a chance of that?"

"He may have. We can make a search later. As I see it, you could be in a strong position with the book should Marta be dead."

"In what way?"

The old man shrugged. "From what I gathered, this book of Marta's was to be sensational in nature. Providing you discover her notes and write the book as she planned it, you could well have the basis for a best seller. And no one can sue Marta for libel or make her take back any maligning statements if she is not alive. The authenticity of the book might be questioned but nothing could be proven."

She stared at him in surprise. "You think the book might be a bigger success with Marta dead?"

"It's possible," he said. "Apart from the fact there's no danger of lawsuits or having to make retractions, there are the added details of her mysterious disappearance. If that is not solved there will be much speculation in the press as to what happened to her. We cannot confine this scandal to the St. Anton police beyond a certain length of time. After that the world press will make the most of it."

Ina gave the old man a troubled look. "When I undertook to work with Marta on the book I assumed it would be no more libelous than the average memoir of a screen star. If it is filled with malicious stories and reputation-destroying facts, I'm not sure I'll want to go on with it."

David Leopold said, "Marta would not let me read the material she'd prepared. But knowing her, I'm sure it is not mild in nature. Still, all this is only conjecture."

"When do you feel we might look for those notes?" she asked.

"Shortly," the old man said. "I wonder that Marta did not send some of the material to you so that you might have an idea what she wanted to produce in the book."

"Nothing was sent me. Unless it arrived after I left," she said.

"Miss Bromley seems to think something was sent you. Perhaps the explanation is that you left before it came in the mail. Service is very slow these days."

"I'm writing my mother every day," Ina told him. "I'll ask in my next letter if any package has arrived from Austria."

"A good idea," David Leopold said. "And if there is anything, she could perhaps return it here."

"I will ask her to do that," Ina promised.

The old man's lined face showed gratitude. "I must thank you for being so patient with me. The truth is I am very confused and upset by all that has happened. Marta saved my life and I shall always be thankful to her for that no matter what differences we may have had along the way."

"Let us hope she returns soon," Ina said quietly.

"Yes," he said with a sigh.

She said good night and went up to her bedroom. She felt sorry for the unhappy man and worried that things were not going to work out as he hoped. She had no idea what had happened to Marta, but the missing woman had been gone quite a long while now. It seemed doubtful that she would return on her own alive and well.

The lights in her room had been turned on, a fire in the fireplace blazed and her bed had been turned down for the night. She closed the door after her and went over to stand before the fireplace and stare into the flames. And as she stood there she once again had that eerie feeling she was being watched. She turned around quickly and stared first at one section of the room and then the other. But her frightened eyes found nothing and the silence was broken only by the crackling of the logs in the fireplace. After a moment she decided to get ready for bed.

A few minutes later she slipped between the sheets and turned off the last of the lights in her bedroom. Now she lay back on her pillow and stared up into the darkness. There was no moon and so no glimmer of moonlight from the windows as there had been on other nights.

She tried to think of pleasant things but her mind kept

returning to the mystery she faced in the old castle. David Leopold claimed that the poison of Karl Bruck still created an evil atmosphere in the castle. And surely the phantom presence of Marta Landen presided over its endless rooms and shadowy corridors. What did it all mean? What sort of macabre puzzle had she become involved in?

She thought she heard a footstep at the other end of the room, near the fireplace. And then a board creaked in a gentle, sinister manner. Her whole body tensed and she sat up in bed to stare in the direction from which the faint sounds had come. But she could see nothing in the shadowy glow of the fire.

Then there came a whisper. A whisper hoarse and clear from the same area of the room. "Ina!"

She gasped. "Who is there?"

"Ina!" the hoarse whisper came again.

"Who are you? What do you want?" she cried out in terror.

"Leave this place!"

"What?"

"Leave this place or you will die!" The whisper faded on the last word of the warning.

Ina reached out a trembling hand to switch on the bedside lamp but it wouldn't go on. She tried again, frantic by now. The light refused to go on as she flicked the switch back and forth. She had only the dull glow from the fireplace to break the darkness of the big bedroom. Panic swept through her and her breathing became strained. Then to add to her horror she saw the door from the corridor opening slowly. Her eyes widened as she watched it come open until there revealed in the corridor was a ghostly figure!

It was the figure of an SS officer in cap and uniform! And as she watched frozen into a motionless silence by this phantom, it started to come toward her. One step at a time the ghostly figure moved into the bedroom, until at last it was at her bedside and she could see the details of the uniform clearly though the face of the apparition was blurred!

A gloved hand reached out for her throat and she finally managed to scream and scream loudly. Then she fell into a faint. And when she opened her eyes again Claude Leopold and Kate Bromley were standing by her bedside.

Claude asked, "What happened?"

She raised herself up in bed, the memory of the horror coming back to her. She gasped, "I heard a voice! Then the door opened and a ghost came into the room!"

The young violinist frowned. "A ghost?"

"Yes. A phantom in the uniform of an SS officer."

Claude turned to Kate Bromley who stood beside him looking formidable in a black dressing gown. He asked, "Did you see anything on your way here?"

"No, sir," the woman said. "I heard a scream and came here at once. The door was closed and when I came inside I found Miss Sperling had fainted."

"And you saw no one?"

"No, sir. I put on the light and then you came," Kate Bromley said.

Memory of her terror in not being able to turn on the lights came back to Ina and she glanced and saw that her bedside lamp was indeed burning brightly. She gave Claude an astonished look. "I tried the light and it wouldn't come on!"

"It's on now," he said. And he turned to the big woman in the black dressing gown. "Did you have any trouble with it?"

"No," she said with a sullen look on her broad face.

Claude gave Ina a sympathetic glance. "Perhaps you were nervous when you awoke and couldn't manage the switch."

"I'm sure I handled it right," Ina insisted. "It wouldn't come on."

He said, "I can't explain it unless the switch is faulty. It's on now and Miss Bromley says she had no problem with the lamp."

Kate Bromley asked, "Will you need me any longer?"

"No," Claude said. "You can go back to your room. I'm sorry you were disturbed."

The big woman merely nodded and marched out of the bedroom. Ina watched her go and then gave a long sigh of resignation. She was already prepared to have her story discredited, sure that her weird experience would be put down to overwrought nerves.

She looked up into Claude's concerned face. "I'm sorry I wakened you," she said.

"It doesn't matter."

"I did hear a weird whisper and see that figure."

Claude looked baffled. "Kate Bromley claims the door was closed when she came in and there was no sign of anyone."

"I knew you wouldn't believe me," she said unhappily.

"It's not that I don't believe you," Claude said, "it's just that there doesn't seem to be any evidence to support your story."

"I did see a man in a Nazi uniform."

Claude's handsome face showed concern. "Don't you think you were influenced by all the stories you've heard about the ghost of Karl Bruck haunting this house?"

"How do you mean?"

"All the ghost stories preyed on your mind and prepared you for something like this. I don't blame you for being in a nervous state, but I don't think you should make too much of it."

She gave him a sober look. "I'm not superstitious and I'm not a fool."

He looked embarrassed. "I didn't mean to suggest you were either."

"Maybe we'd better drop it," she said. "I can see we're not going to agree."

"Better to let it go until the morning," Claude suggested. He hesitated by her bedside. "You're not angry with me?"

"No."

"We'll talk about it in the morning," he promised as he bent over and touched his lips to her forehead. Then with a small smile on his handsome face he left the room.

She lay back on her pillow with a sigh. She knew she had been taunted by the whisper and she had seen that blurred figure even if no one else was willing to believe her. What it meant was another matter. Why was she being made a target of the phantom?

When she awoke the next morning it was snowing. She showered and put on her dressing gown just as the maid arrived with her breakfast tray.

"I see it is snowing," she said to the girl.

"Yes, Miss," the thin maid said as she set out the things from the tray. Then she turned to her apologetically to add, "I'm later this morning, but we have had some trouble downstairs."

"Oh?"

"Yes, Miss," the maid went on in her nervous way. "One of the staff was found dead."

"That's too bad. Who?"

"Hans."

"The old man who supervised the household staff? He let me in the first day I arrived."

The maid nodded. "Yes, Ma'am. He had been at the castle longer than any of the rest of us."

"I'm sure of that," she said. "I have an idea he may have been here during my uncle's day."

"I wouldn't know, Miss."

"What happened to him?"

The maid hesitated. "I think you'd best find that out from Mr. Leopold. We don't know exactly."

"I understand," she said. "Thank you for telling me, anyway."

"Yes, Miss," the girl said and hurried out.

There had been something in the girl's manner which made Ina wonder—an odd kind of uneasiness which had shown itself. Perhaps she had imagined this, but she didn't think so. It was natural that the woman should have been upset by the unexpected death of a colleague. But she felt she'd sensed a hint of something more in the maid's reaction to the death.

This along with her own weird experience of the previous night brought her a feeling of fresh fear. She spent only a short time at breakfast and then went downstairs. When she reached the lower hallway she met Gretchen. The blonde girl was still in a dressing gown and looked as if she'd hurriedly gotten out of bed.

Seeing Ina she said, "The police are here."

"The police? Have they found your mother?"

Gretchen shook her head. "No, it's about something else. My father and brother are in the study talking to them now."

"I see," she said.

Gretchen gave her a knowing look. "We had a death here last night."

"So I heard. It was Hans, wasn't it?"

"Yes."

"I don't know the details," she added.

Gretchen looked bleak. "They're not all that pleasant."

"Oh?"

"They found him in the snow on a hill just behind here. A farmer was driving by in his sleigh early this morning before the storm began and discovered him."

Ina stared at the blonde girl in surprise. "What would Hans be doing out there?"

"No one seems to know. And he had no hat or overcoat on, even thought it was very cold last night."

"Did he die from exposure?"

"No. It seemed he'd been struck down in some way. His head was badly cut and bruised. He died from either shock or brain injuries. And the farmer claimed there were ski tracks coming down the hill past the spot where he found the body."

"Ski tracks?"

"Yes. As if whoever had knocked him down had come upon him on skis."

"That's very strange," Ina said.

"Very," Gretchen agreed dryly. "And there's something else. One of Han's hands was clutching a medal."

Ina frowned. "A medal?"

"Yes," the other girl said, "a German one, an iron cross."

CHAPTER SEVEN

The fears which had existed just below the surface in Ina's mind now rose up uncontrolled. And a picture of an old man beaten and dead in the snow mingled with one of the ghostly SS officer she'd seen standing in her doorway. The stories she'd heard about the cruel Karl Bruck's ghost skiing on the slopes on wintry nights came vividly to her. And she asked herself whether the ghost which had attacked the old man had been the same one she'd seen.

She said, "What could it mean? The medal Hans was clutching in his hand."

"I hardly dare guess," Gretchen said with an air of disgust. "I know the stories it will lead to. Hans will become celebrated because of his weird death. The rumors about an avenging ghost of Karl Bruck on skis will be revived again."

"Perhaps with good reason."

"Who knows?" Gretchen said with one of her mocking smiles. "Perhaps if Mother were here she could tell us. But where is Mother?"

Ina gave the girl a startled glance. "Your mother's disappearance and now this murder! The police must be curious about what has been happening here."

"Possibly."

Ina worried, "I don't want to be standing out here when they go."

"Why be shy? Some of our local police are handsome fellows," Gretchen said in her mocking way.

"I'll go into the drawing room and wait for Claude."

Gretchen said, "I'm going upstairs. I came down without bothering to dress when I heard the news."

"Then I'll see you later," Ina said.

"Yes," Gretchen replied and turned and started up the stairway.

Ina went on down the hall to the drawing room. As she entered the elegant, big room the massive oil painting of Marta Landen caught her attention. She had never realized before how lifelike the study of the screen star was. Its vivid colors were right for the glamorous Marta who was still a romantic figure at an age when she could be a grandmother. Again she wondered where the actress could have gone.

She was still standing there considering the painting when she heard someone behind her and turned to see that it was Claude. The handsome young violinist looked troubled.

She said, "What did you find out?"

"Nothing, really," he said with a sigh. "We were giving information rather than receiving it. They wanted our version about finding the body."

"Poor Hans!"

"I know," he said. "He was the most trustworthy servant we had. Father will be lost without him. Hans was here before Father married Marta."

"I'm sure he'll be missed," she agreed. "He was in charge of the household when my Uncle Ralph was alive. When Marta wrote the account of his drowning she mentioned that Hans had been the first to find his body in the stream."

"With Marta gone and Hans dead this will be a difficult place for my father to cope with," Claude said with a worried air.

"Who do they think killed Hans?"

"They have no suspects," he said gloomily. "They seem to think it may have been an accident. Few people ski at night and some of those who do take to the slopes do it on a drunken wager. They have an idea someone fairly drunk might have come down that hill and happened on old Hans."

This struck her as a very prosaic explanation but she made no comment. Instead she asked another question. "What was Hans doing out in the cold night without a hat or coat?"

"That's also a puzzler," Claude said.

"It would almost seem that something sent him out of the house," she suggested. "Suppose he saw this skier outside and for one reason or another wanted to talk to him."

"You mean he might have recognized someone out there and decided to question him before he got away?" Claude said.

"Yes," she agreed. "Or there could have been someone so strange that he went out to investigate."

Claude gave her a wise glance. "You're thinking that it might have been the ghost?"

"Some odd figure," she said carefully.

"I don't agree."

"What about the medal that was found in his hand?"

The young violinist looked uncomfortable. "I don't know. Maybe he had it in his hand before he went outside. He had a son who was killed early in the war and I believe he won several awards."

"You think it could have been his son's then?"

"It's beyond my explaining at the moment," Claude said.

Her eyes met his. "Something like the ghost in that respect."

"Only the ignorant locals deal in that ghost talk," he warned her. "I can promise you the police won't be impressed by it. They know that Bruck met his death with Hitler in Berlin, and when a man is dead he doesn't return."

"Perhaps not," she said. "But one can almost picture the old man battling with the phantom skier and tearing the iron cross from him."

"We'll discuss it later."

It was an unsatisfactory answer but she hadn't expected much better. The way things were now, the death of Hans would likely be listed as an accident and the culprit in the matter some drunken skier. It was too pat! Especially when they chose to overlook the iron medal found in Hans' possession.

She had tried to draw Claude out more on the subject but it was a touchy one with him. He'd be anxious for the police to get away from the castle as soon as possible.

Claude said, "I have a few things to do in connection with Hans' death. I will have to go into the village. But I should be back early."

"I'll see you then," she said quietly. And glancing at the impressive painting of Marta, she said, "So now we have two unsolved mysteries."

Claude frowned. "I'd hardly call the tragic accident which happened to Hans a mystery." And with that he left her alone in the drawing room once again.

She moved across to windows which looked out on the front driveway of the estate. And she saw Claude walking toward the parking area, his head bent down against the driving snow. It looked as if there might be quite a heavy snowfall. She felt a sudden pang of loneliness and fear.

With Claude away from the place she was doubly uneasy. She stared out at the falling snow and a few minutes later saw his car round the corner of the castle and drive away. She had come to like the talented adopted son of Marta and David a great deal. No wonder they were proud of him. He had so many fine qualities. Yet even he wanted to avoid any discussion of the ghost or to say anything that might indicate the death of Hans had occurred under mysterious circumstances.

She was standing with her back to the room considering this when she heard someone coming up behind her. She turned and saw that it was David Leopold, a troubled expression on his lined old face. The gray-haired man was garbed in one of his dark sedate suits and his face mirrored the strain he'd been under.

He said, "You've heard about Hans?"

"Yes. It's too bad."

"Very sad," the old man said with a deep sigh. "He was already employed here when I came after my marriage to Marta."

"You will miss him, I'm sure."

"I won't know what to do without him," David Leopold told her earnestly. "And if Marta comes back and finds out what happened to him, I'm sure she'll never forgive me."

"But you can't be blamed."

"Marta would not see it that way," the old man worried.

"Why do you think he went out in the night without waiting to put on a hat or overcoat?" she wondered.

A frown creased Leopold's forehead. He said, "I think he heard a cry perhaps. Or it may be that he looked out and saw something that upset him. He evidently hurried from the house for some reason."

"It would have to be something like that," she said. "He was very devoted to Marta. Could it have been she whom he thought he saw?"

David Leopold blinked. "That had not occurred to me. But if he had seen her out there after her being missing, I have no doubt that is exactly how he would have reacted."

"I doubt if it was Marta."

"Who can tell?"

She asked, "Did the police link her disappearance with his death in any way?"

"No," the old man said. "But they didn't hit on the possibility which you brought up just now, nor did I. It is very interesting."

"It was just a thought," she said. "I don't think you should take it seriously."

"Yet, who knows?" David Leopold said thoughtfully and stared out at the snow. "Quite a bit of time has passed now since Marta vanished."

"Aren't the police getting more concerned?"

The old man shrugged. "They have so many problems."

"I suppose they do, but Marta's life is just as important as any."

"I fully agree," David Leopold said. "I keep thinking of the material she was working on. The facts she was gathering to have ready for you. And I still wonder if she didn't actually mail you some of it before you left for here."

"I've written my mother to ask her about that."

The old man nodded. "You will understand I'm very concerned. I would like to relieve my mind on the matter. Would you be good enough to phone your mother and ask her if any such package of material was sent you. That would settle it."

She stared at him. "You really want me to do that?"

"Why not?" he asked. "Trans-Atlantic calls are common these days. I frequently make them in connection with business. It would be early morning there now. Would she be at home?"

"Mother rarely leaves the apartment in the morning," Ina said.

"Then go to my study and place the call," he said. "In a few minutes you'll have the joy of hearing your mother's voice and we'll know for certain if my dear Marta sent her any such material."

"If you like," she said, still amazed that he should be so anxious about it.

"I feel it important," he explained. "If we know that all the notes she made are here, you can then begin assembling and working on them. Otherwise you are wasting your time."

"You feel I should go ahead with the book whether Marta returns or not, if I find enough material?"

"I think so," he said. "It would be a suitable memorial for Marta if nothing else."

"Very well," Ina said. "I'll call Mother."

He went with her to the study and she sat in his chair at the big desk and placed the phone call through the overseas operator in Vienna. The call was transferred to Paris and from there to New York. She waited tensely as the operators coolly relayed information and then the phone in the New York apartment rang and her mother answered it.

Ina felt a wave of relief on hearing her mother's voice; she said, "It's Ina. I'm calling from St. Anton in Austria."

"I don't believe it!" her mother gasped. "You sound so clear and near."

"I'm talking to you from across the ocean," she said. "How are you?"

"Lonely and worried about you," her mother said. "I do hope you'll soon be coming back."

"Soon."

"How is Marta?"

She knew she had to keep up the pretence that she had met the glamorous film star. She said, "As usual. There's a question I have to ask. One of the secretaries here mailed out some material and we think it may have gone to my address in New York by error. Did you receive any such package?"

"No," her mother said. "Only a few letters have arrived. The mail has been very light."

"You're sure?" she persisted. "There have been no large envelopes postmarked Austria?"

"None," her mother said. "If there had been, I would have surely noticed."

"Very well, then," she said. "I'll be writing to you as usual and I'll get back as quickly as possible."

"Ina, there's nothing wrong?" Her mother sounded worried.

"Of course not. Why?"

"I mean your calling this way. And you sound very tense."

"That's the long-distance," she said "Everything is all right. Don't you worry. Now I must hang up. Goodbye, Mother!"

She put down the phone with a sigh and glanced at David Leopold, who had been standing across the desk from her. She said, "There was no letter from here. No package, not anything!"

The gray-haired man listened with interest. "Then that means all the material is here in the castle. I see no reason why you shouldn't begin to work on it."

"If you're sure Marta won't be angry if and when she should come back."

His eyes met hers in a solemn glance. "I will make a confession to you," he said. "I'm beginning to lose hope that she is going to return."

"I'm sorry."

"It must be faced," the old man said. "I can only hope she has not suffered some violent fate. I do not dare to think of that side of it."

"When do you want me to start sorting out Marta's notes and other items?" Ina asked him.

He made an expansive gesture. "Why not now?"

"I'll be glad to get on with it," she admitted.

"Then you have my permission to go to her room and sort out the contents of the desk up there," the old man said. "I would appreciate having a daily report from you on the progress you've made and also as to what you've found."

"I'll do that," she promised.

David Leopold started for the hallway, "I'll have the housekeeper provide you with a key to that room and escort you up there."

She stood in the library waiting as he went to locate the housekeeper. She imagined that things would be in a state of chaos as the result of Hans' death. He had looked after all the management of the domestic staff. Now there would have to be a complete change.

Ina found herself both pleased and a little let down with David's decision to allow her to begin sorting out his wife's papers. It was the moment she'd been waiting for, but she'd expected Marta to be on hand to guide and help her. Now it would be a much more tedious and lonely task. She was very anxious to do the book on Marta's life though she hoped it would not be too sensational. She also felt she must solve this new puzzle of what had become of Marta Landen in order to produce a satisfactory book about the star's career.

But nothing seemed to be happening in Marta's case to clear up the mystery. And now there was a new mystery to be solved. There was no doubt that Hans had been the victim of someone's violence, but had the violence been accidental or intentional?

She was interrupted in her deliberations by the arrival of the housekeeper and David Leopold. The old man seemed in a very earnest mood as he spoke briefly in German to the housekeeper before he turned to speak to Ina.

He told her, "My wife's room adjoins mine. I have no idea how well her papers are in order. She has a kneehole desk in the corner of her bedroom and she usually worked there with a portable typewriter. Probably you will find most of her notes there."

"Thank you," she said.

"Mrs. Horst will take you to Marta's room," David Leopold said. "Do not feel you must hurry with the task. Just take a look around this afternoon if you prefer. But at least this will be a start. If Marta returns I'm sure she will forgive us intruding on her this way."

"I hope so," she said.

Mrs. Horst, a placid-looking middle-aged woman with gray hair parted in the middle and pulled back, led the way up the stairs. She halted at the second floor and took Ina down a hallway to the rear of the castle. There she unlocked a door and opened it for her without a word. Then she handed her the key and with a brief nod was on her way.

Ina entered the room which Marta had used all her years as mistress of the castle. There was a strong odor of perfume in the air as if someone had just passed through the room wearing a scent. It gave her a kind of eerie sensation to know that this was Marta's perfume and the room was still very much alive with it.

How long had it been since Marta had used the room? Quite a number of days now. The drapes had been left drawn and she went over and opened them, thinking it would make the room less macabre. It was still snowing outside and the room seemed just about as weird as it had in shadow. She saw the desk which David Leopold had referred to and noticed there was a confusion of papers on its surface.

She went over to it and lifted up some of the several sheets to read. Some of them were letters and others had been filled with data for the proposed biography. It would mean a good deal of sorting to get all of them in order. She sat in the chair by the desk and checked each of its drawers. Most of them contained materials of some sort pertaining to the book.

In one drawer she discovered files of newspaper clippings including reviews of Marta's plays and films. In another she was faced with a huge folio of correspondence which the star had received over the years and thought important enough to keep. And so it went, each of the drawers contributing to the grand total.

She sat back in the chair with a sigh. It was too late in the day to begin this task. It was something she'd prefer to get at first thing in the morning when her enthusiasm was fresh. She was also reluctant to begin sorting the papers until she was more positive that Marta wouldn't return. She felt the star should lead in the culling of the material.

There was a large colored photograph of Marta on the wall in some kind of Spanish costume. Ina thought it was probably a still from one of her films which had been enlarged and framed. It was a flattering study and probably at least twenty or thirty years old. The girl in the portrait was a sunny twenty, while Marta was now in her fifties.

The perfume in the room did not assault her nostrils as strongly now but it still gave a sensation of some ghostly creature having been there recently. Was Marta dead and had her spirit somehow returned to this room? It was no more weird a thought than to believe that the elderly Hans had been beaten to death by the spirit of the cruel Karl Bruck.

The personalities who had lived in the castle in the past still seemed to dominate the place. Soon the word of Marta's disappearance would get around, and this together with the violent death of Hans would start a new lot of rumors about ghosts. At the moment Ina didn't know whether she believed in their existence or not. But surely she had a strange sort of feeling about these papers.

It was as if an unseen phantom were watching her and trying to restrain her from going through these papers on Marta's desk. She had this feeling and could not seem to throw it off. Was Marta in that room with her and watching her? She hoped not. With a sigh she bent over the desk again and began separating the papers by subject matter.

The room had a high ceiling and was surprisingly drab in decor. She would have expected Marta to have something much more lively. But the actress might have preferred this quieter atmosphere for her life here with her husband. In many ways Marta's life had been tragic. Even her associations with the Nazis had ended in disaster with the collapse of Germany and the deaths of so many of its leaders, including her special friend, Karl Bruck.

She continued sorting out the various papers as these thoughts rambled through her mind. And she became familiar with Marta's large scrawling handwriting, as most of the sheets were signed by her or entirely written in her generously formed script.

Many of the pages were devoted to typed opinions of Marta's concerning various personalities in the theatre and screen world. Ina found some of them clever and interesting while others were either of little importance or referred to people of whom the vast majority of the public had never heard.

Gradually she was getting some order out of the chaos she'd found on the top of the desk. It seemed strange to her that Marta would leave the material in such a mess and she wondered if perhaps someone else had quickly gone through it to see what she had written. It was entirely possible. But whom? Some maid or perhaps Gretchen. She would be the most likely suspect since she'd had little love for her mother.

Ina had reached the last of one confused assortment of the letters and was going to begin another when she came on a sheet of notepaper in Marta's familiar writing. She read it and then read it again with a frown coming to her attractive face.

"To begin another year with fear," the note in the star's big scrawl read, "but to hope that I shall one day regain my position in the film world and find peace of mind. With the book—" And here the note ended abruptly, as if the writer had been interrupted or had simply risen from the desk with it unfinished. Why had she written it and who had she written it to?

Ina stared at the short note which was somewhat like a message from the dead. She had begun to feel that Marta was dead. She knew she could be wrong, but somehow this thought forced itself on her. Even David Leopold was beginning to lose faith that she would return. The fact that he'd opened the room almost proved that.

She knew that Claude was also badly worried about his mother's fate, and only Gretchen was cold and uncaring about what had happened. Though some of the things the blonde girl had said recently had hinted that for all her battling with Marta she was missing her. It was a strange relationship that existed between the mother and daughter.

Ina got up from the desk with the unfinished note in her hand, and feeling that she had come upon a find she turned and left the room that spoke so loudly of the missing Marta Landen. She went downstairs to the study where she hoped she might find David Leopold. And as she'd anticipated he was sitting at his desk. She went into the room and took a stand before him.

The gray-haired man looked up with mild interest. "Yes, Miss Sperling?"

"I made a start with the papers," she said.

"Good."

"And I found something."

His eyebrows lifted. "Indeed?"

"Yes. It's an unfinished note written by Marta. I thought you might like to see it. I don't know whether it has any importance or not." She handed him the note.

He frowned at it. "It really doesn't say much of anything," he finally commented.

"You will notice in the first sentence she uses the word fear," Ina pointed out. "Why should she use that word rather than boredom, impatience, resignation or even frustration? It seems to indicate more concern about her career than seems justified."

David Leopold placed the sheet of paper down and then drummed the fingers of one hand on it. "I see what you mean," he said.

"It caught my attention because it didn't seem the right word for that sentence."

David Leopold's lined face showed troubled thought. "Still it might be. She was very much afraid that she'd never work again or at least never regain the position she'd once held in the film world."

"You think she was referring to fear of failure?"

"What else?"

"I thought it could point to some other fear. And that whatever she feared might have led to her vanishing."

The elderly man shook his head. "No, I'm afraid I can't agree with you on this. Though I do thank you for bringing my attention to it. It shows you're taking your work seriously."

"I promise that I'm doing that," she said. "And I'm sorry to have bothered you with this."

"Not at all," he said. "I'll gladly discuss any of your findings at any time."

"I sorted out a lot of material in the short while I was up there," she said.

"Go in and work whenever you like," David Leopold advised.

"I'll get what I find in order," she suggested. "Then we can discuss whether I should return to New York and work on the material there. Of course if Marta should turn up that would change it all and I'd prefer to stay on here."

"Let us leave it to your good judgment," the old man said.

"Thank you for your confidence."

"I know Marta trusted you implicitly or she would never have sent for you. And you are Gretchen's cousin. I consider it good of you to remain here in the face of this puzzling business and the unpleasantness you have known while in this house."

She smiled wanly. "One learns to take such things in their stride."

"You have been very good about it," the old man said seriously. "And now this tragic business of Hans makes it more difficult."

"I hope they find who killed him."

"We all do that," the old man agreed. "Even if it were an accident, it was a most cowardly thing to run off and leave him to die in the snow."

"It's hard to conceive it being an accident," she said.

"That's the police's theory, not mine," David Leopold told her. "I see the snow is letting up so at least we may have more pleasant weather."

"I'll not take up any more of your time," she said, sensing that he was becoming uneasy. And she excused herself and left him to return to whatever work he was doing at his desk.

She went on back to the hall and then paused by the drawing room. She'd only been there a moment when the vivacious Gretchen came to join her, dressed in a powder blue pants suit with a white blouse and large blue satin tie.

The blonde girl said, "I've been looking for you."

"I was in your mother's room."

Gretchen showed surprise. "What were you doing there?"

"Your father decided it was time for me to begin sifting through the papers she'd gathered."

"I see."

"I worked over an hour and got quite a lot done," she said.

Gretchen said, "You work too hard. That's why I wanted to see you. I've decided to go over to the Post Hotel for the tea dance and I wondered if you'd enjoy going?"

She showed hesitation. "Tea dance?"

"Yes. It's an afternoon dance for the skiers and those

staying at the hotels as ordinary guests. But you don't have to dress in any formal fashion."

"It sounds pleasant," she said cautiously, "but I don't think I should go."

"Why not?"

"I have work here."

"It's too late to work now," Gretchen said. "It will soon be time for dinner. The dance is usually a fun thing. I'm sure you'll have a good time if you come with me."

Ina still hesitated. "Won't you be criticized for going out to a party with Hans found dead only this morning?"

"I mean no disrespect to Hans," Gretchen said. "And I'm sure no one will think anything about it. And if you come along I'll tell you all kinds of personal things about Mother which might put some spice in your book."

This last was a bait too tempting to resist. Ina gave in and agreed to join Gretchen. She went upstairs and put on a long afternoon gown and then met the blonde girl in the front hall. They went out together and there was an awkward silence between them for a little while.

As they settled comfortably in the station wagon Gretchen suddenly asked her, "What were you doing in Mother's room?"

"Your father wants me to go over all the papers she had for her book. I imagine most of them are in or on her desk in the bedroom."

"So that's it," Gretchen said, a strange look on her face. "It begins to seem he doesn't expect her back."

"I'm sure he's worried about it."

"He probably misses Mother ordering him about," was Gretchen's comment.

"I'm sure they must have been close," she said.

"You didn't live here. What could you know about it?"

Ina felt her cheeks warm. "I was just assuming it."

"You shouldn't assume anything," the other girl said in her most sarcastic manner as they drove the road to the village. "Not if you're going to write that book about Mother."

"Why do you say that?"

"Because it's true. You need to dig and search out the facts. And one fact is that Mother ruled the castle mercilessly. Everyone obeyed her. At any rate everyone but me."

"Was she that difficult and overbearing?"

"You've heard the term temperamental in connection with actors and actresses, haven't you?" Gretchen asked as she drove along with her eyes fixed on the plowed white road ahead.

"Yes."

"Well, Mother could have created the word. She was the most temperamental person I've ever known."

"Yet her husband and Claude seem to adore her," Ina pointed out.

An expression of distaste crossed the face of the blonde girl whose beauty was so much like her mother's. She said, "David has always been grateful because she married him. And Claude came to us an orphan. So he has reason to be thankful to her as well."

"You felt nothing for your mother?" she asked. If Gretchen's advice was to dig, why not begin with her.

"I felt hatred for her a lot of the time," the blonde said. "I still do."

They were nearing the outskirts of the village and passed the same quaint church with the onion-like top to its steeple. She said, "You sound as if you were proud of it."

"Of hating her?"

"Yes."

"I am."

"Why?"

Gretchen gave her a brief, bitter smile. "Can't you guess?"

"No."

"Because it made me my own person. I didn't bow down to her or worship her as her fans did. I stood up to her and battled with her and did my own thing. Perhaps in the end she liked me better than the others for doing that."

She said, "That's an interesting speculation."

Gretchen's pretty face had clouded. "And maybe when

it comes right down to it I cared more for her than either my stepfather or adopted brother."

Ina said, "I've wondered about that."

"You have? Why?"

"Certain things you said. Small give-aways. You try to appear hard and cold but I don't think you really are like that."

She slowed the speed of the station wagon as they reached the parking lot of the big hotel. Then turning expertly in the freshly plowed roadway, she brought the car to a halt in line with rows of other vehicles. The hotel itself was like an over-sized English Tudor mansion with the familiar siding and tiny windows.

Gretchen turned off the motor of the car and gave Ina a look of interest. "I'm surprised that you've been watching me so closely. I must be careful from now on."

Ina smiled. "I'm your cousin and your friend. At least I hope you'll allow me to be your friend."

"A friend is something I can use," Gretchen said, staring at her.

"Oh?"

"I haven't that many."

"I'm sorry."

"I've lived in that big house and fought the good fight with Mother. I've been a lonely person. Most of the friends I made she stole from me. Rolf for example."

"Was he truly a friend?"

"No," Gretchen admitted. "But he was a kind of substitute. He was company and he could be fun when he liked."

"I'm sure he has charm."

"He has. He'll be here this afternoon."

"Inside?"

"Yes."

"What about his instructor job?"

"He takes two days a week to himself. This happens to be one of them."

Ina gave her a knowing look. "And that is why you wanted to attend the afternoon dance?"

"No. I won't talk to him at all. I'll leave him to you. He and I aren't friends any more because of my mother."

"I didn't realize it was so definite."

"It is," the blonde girl said. "But I'll have other young men to dance with. There are a lot of visitors here I know."

"I'm glad," she said.

"One thing," Gretchen said as they got out of the station wagon.

"What?"

"Be careful with Rolf."

"You think he's dangerous?"

"He can be. He's well aware of his charm," Gretchen said as they walked together to the entrance of the hotel. "And he'll try to exert it on you."

"I'm prepared for that," she said.

Gretchen gave her a solemn look. "And don't forget he's probably responsible for my mother's disappearance and likely her death."

CHAPTER EIGHT

Ina stared at her cousin. "Why do you say that?"

"I think the call she received that night was from Rolf."

"And?"

"She probably planned to meet him for their own private New Year's celebration. But when she went out there it wasn't Rolf who was waiting for her but someone else."

"Who?"

"I have no idea," Gretchen said. "But I'm reasonably sure there was another person and that person was the one who either kidnapped her or murdered her."

They were standing by the entrance of the hotel. Ina asked, "Have you talked this over with Rolf?"

Gretchen shook her head. "I've already told you we're not on friendly terms."

"But in a case like this?"

The blonde girl smiled coldly. "Mother created the situation so I'm making no exception for her."

"It could be a mistake."

"I'll risk that," Gretchen replied.

"You're making me feel awkward about meeting him before I go in there," Ina protested.

"No need," her cousin said. "I just felt you should know all the circumstances."

"But all this is guessing on your part rather than facts," Ina said.

Gretchen gave her a knowing glance. "I think what I've told you comes close to the truth."

They went on inside. Ina was in a thoroughly confused state of mind. She was beginning to have suspicions that Gretchen knew a lot more about her mother's disappearance than she had yet told. Perhaps she knew all about it. In the meanwhile she was just dropping a hint of what had happened when it suited her.

The hotel was busy with many skiers in the lobby. Most of them were in their late teens or early twenties with a scattering of older people. English and French seemed to be spoken primarily, although Ina's ear caught a few other languages as they crossed the lobby together. As usual Gretchen drew a lot of attention. There were unabashed stares in their direction by a good proportion of the young males and some audible comments followed them as they started down a broad hallway.

Gretchen smiled at her triumphantly. "I like to make my entrance about this time. Most of the crowd gather here at this hour."

They went on to the end of the hall to the entrance of the lounge. It was another large room with a bar, a huge fireplace and a circular dancing area in front of it. The floor of the lounge was marble and the general décor was dark wood and leather. The place was already well-filled, even busier than the lobby.

A lot of the patrons were lined up at the long bar, which ran the length of the room. A few were at tables and several couples, dressed in ski outfits, were dancing. The rear wall of the room was all glass and gave an excellent view of the mountains and the ski-lifts and buildings.

Gretchen halted and surveyed the room. Then she waved to a young man standing at the bar; a blond, pleasant man who returned the wave and came striding toward them.

Gretchen said, "He's English and nice. Here is where you and I part. You look up Rolf."

"If I can find him," Ina said.

"That won't be hard," Gretchen said. "Just search out

the prettiest girl in the room and Rolf will likely be at her side."

The young Englishman had joined them and said, "Gretchen, what a nice surprise. I thought you'd deserted me!"

Gretchen smiled. "I've been busy." She turned to Ina, "Ina I'd like you to meet Jack Land. Jack, this is my cousin from America, Ina Sperling."

Jack gave her a warm smile. "Delighted, Ina. I'm amazed that you're so dark compared to Gretchen."

Gretchen spoke up quickly, "Our family is filled with contrasting types. Ina has a date, so we'll go off and have that chat we'd planned."

"Excellent," the young man said. And he smiled Ina's way again. "Good meeting you, Ina." Then he and Gretchen went off to a table near the glass wall. Gretchen offered Ina a mocking smile in farewell.

Ina stood just inside of the door of the lounge debating whether to retreat or not. Gretchen had played a neat trick on her, asking her to go to the dance, and then escaping from her at the first opportunity. It was typical of the striking blonde. No wonder she and Marta had not gotten on well, their personalities would be bound to be in conflict.

She turned her gaze to the orchestra, three men in native Tyrolean costume including the traditional leather pants, playing an accordion, a zither and a saxophone. The music was cheery and tuneful and the couples on the floor appeared to be enjoying it.

The lounge was filled with talk and laughter as the orchestra played on almost continuously. She had decided to go back to the lobby and leave the merry-makers when suddenly from a dark corner of the room the tall, craggy-faced Rolf Monner appeared. The ski instructor was smiling as he came toward her.

As he joined her, he said, "What an unexpected pleasure. I was going to call you at the castle."

She smiled. "I doubt if you even remember my name."

He showed a mouthful of white teeth as he laughed and said, "Ina! Ina Sperling!"

"You must have a system for remembering," she said.

"In your case it was no problem. You have a great deal of charm, Ina."

She gave him a wise look. "I've been told about you and your methods for turning a girl's head."

He laughed again. "You mustn't believe any of it. This is the beginning of the *Fasching* season and almost every evening there are parties."

"We've not been in a party mood at the castle," she told him.

He turned serious. "I can understand. How did you get here this afternoon?"

"Gretchen brought me and then deserted me almost the moment we arrived."

"That does not surprise me," the ski instructor said. "Where is she now?"

"With some Englishman named Jack Land. Do you know him?"

"I've heard of him," Rolf Monner said. And at that moment the musical trio began to play a lilting waltz. He smiled at her and asked, "Wouldn't you like to dance? That music is very good."

"Thank you," she said.

"I have a table just across from here," he told her. "You can leave your coat and cap there." And he escorted her across the room to a table for two. She had half expected to see some other girl seated at it but the chairs were empty. She quickly put her things on one of them and then they returned to the dance floor.

More couples had gotten up to enjoy the traditional music of the mountainous Austrian country. Soon she found herself being whirled around the room breathlessly to a typical Viennese waltz. Rolf was a fine dancer and seemed to enjoy it thoroughly.

At last the music ended with a show of applause from the many couples on the floor. She and Rolf went back to his table and she smiled up at him as he helped her into her chair. "I had fun," she said. "I haven't danced a Viennese waltz in ages."

"You made a fine partner," he said, still standing by. "What would you like to drink?"

"How about beer? Some nice dark beer," she said.

"I know just the kind you'll like," he told her and he left to go to the bar.

She relaxed at the table and was pleased to note that they were situated a little way back from the bar and sort of behind the dance area. The orchestra was over at the other side of the fireplace so the music wasn't too loud. At the moment they were taking a break. She gazed down at the other end of the long lounge to see if she could see any sign of Gretchen. But she couldn't spot her at all. It seemed that the blonde girl and her friend had gone off somewhere.

She was contemplating this when a smug-looking Rolf came back carrying steins of beer for them both. He placed hers before her and then sat down, moving his chair so that they were as close together as possible. Then he raised his stein and said, "To my lovely American!"

Ina lifted her own glass with a roguish light in her eyes. "I wonder how many times you've offered that toast before."

"But this is the first!" he protested, sipping his beer.

She shook her head. "You don't even expect me to believe that."

He was smiling. "Do you like the beer?"

"Yes. It's excellent," she said.

"A local brew which I prefer," he told her.

The orchestra had begun playing again and some couples got up to do a lively polka. It was all very gay and like the Austria Ina had looked forward to; quite different from the gray air of suspense and terror she'd left at the castle.

The German had a questioning expression on his long, narrow face. He said, "You're suddenly in a different mood. What is wrong?"

"I was thinking about the castle."

Rolf's eyes met hers. "I hear that Hans was found dead in the snow this morning."

"Under what I'd call mysterious circumstances," she said. "But according to what I've heard, the police seem ready to put it down to an unfortunate accident."

The blond man said, "You don't agree?"

"I think there has to be more to it than that. He was found clutching a German medal in his hand, the iron cross."

"I'm familiar with the decoration," he said dryly. "And I knew Hans."

"You did? I wasn't aware of that," she said. "I'd only seen him a few times since I arrived. But he seemed very pleasant, though he must have been old."

"He was old," Rolf agreed. "In fact his son served in the German army in the Second World War with my father. We used to meet in one of the village taverns and talk about those days."

"Do you know if his son won the iron cross?"

Rolf looked surprised. "Why do you ask that?"

"I wondered if the iron cross he was found holding might have been his son's?"

The tall, blond man was silent for a moment as if the news had really upset him. "I wouldn't know about that," he said quietly.

"I can't believe they would be all that common."

Rolf frowned. "My father won an iron cross but I can't recall Hans ever telling me that his son had that decoration. And they were in the same company, my father and his son."

"You would have expected him to mention it."

"Yes. I know someone else who won the same medal, Otto Fess."

"I didn't know he'd been in the army," she said.

"You've met him?"

"Yes," she said. "Both he and his wife. They came to visit the castle one evening. David Leopold had them for dinner."

"They were friends of Marta's," Rolf agreed. "Pauline

138

was an actress once. Of course she's a lot older than Marta."

"I guessed that. And her husband is fairly old."

"He still could have served in the army. They were taking men of all ages. It was a desperate struggle toward the end."

"You were much too young for that," she said.

"I was born the year the war ended," Rolf Monner said, his face shadowed. "But I heard about it all from my father. He was blinded in one of the last battles. He died only five years ago. So he had plenty of time to tell me about it."

"I'm sorry," she said.

Rolf smiled in his smug way. "Well, I have managed. But I never forget I am a German."

"Was Hans very patriotic?"

"Why wouldn't he be? He lost his son before the war ended."

"Then he would feel strongly about it," she said.

"He did. He always privately expressed the opinion that Marta had turned her back on the German people in their hour of disaster. And he didn't approve of her marriage to David Leopold or of her adopting Claude."

"Still he stayed on in the house?"

"He was very devoted to Marta in spite of his feelings of anger at some of the things she did. And he had strong roots at the castle. He'd been employed there since the time when Karl Bruck bought it."

Her eyebrows raised. "I understood that it was Marta who bought the castle."

"You are wrong," he said. "It was Bruck. As one of those at the helm of the Hitler party he had access to plenty of money. The castle was his gift to Marta and it has lasted to see him only a memory."

"Some think his ghost may have struck Hans down, and the iron medal in the old man's hands had been torn from the coat of the ghost!"

Rolf smiled grimly. "It does make a good ghost story."

"But you don't believe it?"

"I think not."

The music had become more sentimental and the dancing slower. She looked at her half-finished stein of black beer and said, "How do you account for his going out without a hat or coat in the cold night? And where did the medal in his hand come from? Who beat him so badly that he died out there in the snow?"

Rolf avoided looking at her directly, but said, "I think all that will be settled in time."

"That's what they keep saying at the castle but nothing is solved," she said. "Marta hasn't returned."

"I know," Rolf Monner said. "The music is really good now. We should dance." He got her on the floor once more for a lively foxtrot. He danced as well as before but she enjoyed it less. She was convinced that he was deliberately dancing to avoid any further talk about Marta. But she intended to pursue that line of questioning if possible.

When the music ended they returned to the table. Rolf got himself another stein of beer but she wanted no more. He sat staring at her with an amused look. "You don't trust me, do you? I suppose Gretchen told you a lot of rubbish."

"What makes you so sure?"

"Your manner. Every so often you suddenly become very reserved."

"I hadn't realized."

"It's so."

"What is the situation between you and Gretchen?"

He shrugged. "She's too possessive. A man in my line of work makes many friends."

"But wasn't your main argument about Marta?"

The big man hesitated. He took a sip of his beer and stared moodily at the dance floor. "She didn't like my being friendly with Marta. But her mother had more sophistication than Gretchen could ever hope for."

"A little old for you, perhaps?"

"When a man was with Marta he never thought of age."

She gave him a close scrutiny. "You sound as if you had been in love with Marta."

"If I ever loved a woman I'd say it was Marta."

"Didn't you call her on New Year's Eve and ask her to meet you?"

He at once looked wary. "What gave you that idea?"

"There was a call. Gretchen suggests it was you."

Rolf Monner shook his head. "No. It was not me."

"Who then?"

"How should I know?" he asked. "Marta knew literally thousands of people. Why should it have to be me who called at that time?"

Ina said, "Gretchen claims you made a habit of calling and that Marta often went out to join you."

The young man looked annoyed. "Gretchen is trying to make a case against me because she hates me. You shouldn't believe anything she tells you."

"Someone made the call."

"So?"

"Marta vanished and she hasn't been seen since."

"Probably Gretchen was the one behind the call," the ski instructor said. "How do you know that she didn't arrange it and have her mother lured out to a murderer. She hated her enough!"

"You think she'd be capable of that?"

He nodded. "I do. Don't you?"

A cold chill went through her as she looked into his eyes and heard his words of indictment spoken so casually. She said, "Gretchen is a creature of surprises. Often I don't know what to think about her. But for a mother to be murdered by her own daughter seems a little far-fetched."

"It has happened. And the relationship between Gretchen and Marta was no simple daughter and mother thing. They were like rivals. And the fact Marta had lost some of her screen fame and was desperate to keep her control over men made her doubly malevolent."

"You saw some of it."

"It was my misfortune," the German ski instructor said. "I tried to get away from them both. The whole thing was getting attention from the people here and my employers do not like me involved in any scandal."

"Where did David Leopold fit in all this?"

Rolf showed a wry expression. "Where has he ever fitted in Marta's life? What consideration has she ever shown him?"

"She married him."

"Because he was a survivor of a concentration camp and she wanted it known that she sympathized with the unfortunates who had met their deaths in those camps. It paid her to be known in this light. David Leopold was a convenience just as that adopted son was. They were window dressing for her to establish herself in England and America again, and you must give her credit. It worked."

"You think this was all pretence on her part?"

He gave her a grim smile. "Have you met that woman she employed as her companion, Kate Bromley? The big one. There is a character for you. Kate Bromley was an English Nazi and for her Hitler was never wrong. Do you think Marta would have had her around if she hadn't felt the same way."

"Then you're saying that the only man Marta ever loved was Karl Bruck?"

"I think she was happiest with him. And her big days as a star were when she was the idol of Hitler's Germany. She was never as great an attraction again."

"Bruck died in Berlin, didn't he?"

"Yes. Marta confessed to me that her heart died with him," Rolf Monner said. "She told me that much without saying any more. But you can understand that everything else she did was to save her career."

"She married my uncle after that."

Rolf showed interest. "The American playwright. She discussed him with me."

Ina was at once more interested. "What did she say about him?"

"I gather she liked him to a degree. She admired his talent as a playwright and he fathered Gretchen, which was a mixed blessing as far as Marta was concerned. But gradually he and Marta began to have opposing views about politics. He was very anti-Hitler and she preferred to be considered neutral in her views. They quarreled about this."

"There was to have been an anti-Hitler play produced," Ina said. "And then my uncle drowned suddenly and nothing more was heard of it. The script was never sent to New York."

"Knowing Marta and her views I'd say she destroyed it after his drowning," the ski instructor said.

"Did she ever discuss that accident with you?"

"No. She didn't seem to want to talk about it and I could understand that."

"I suppose so," she said. "You know it was Hans who found my uncle's body in the stream."

"And this morning someone else found the body of Hans," Rolf said.

"We're talking about a lot of ghosts," she sighed. "People of the past. Though David Leopold still seems to cling to the hope Marta may still be alive."

"Why should he care? He'd be better off without her."

Ina gave the ski instructor a reproving look. "You're ruling out the fact that he may truly love Marta."

"In that case he's a fool as well as a martyr."

She said, "Did you find yourself sympathetic to Marta's political views?"

He smiled. "Are you asking me if I admire the Hitler legend. For you, the answer is yes. For strangers it is something quite different. My father lost his eyes for the cause just as Hans' son lost his life. There are some things one has to believe in."

"I suppose I shouldn't have asked."

"No. You shouldn't have."

"I came here to write about Marta and her early days in Germany. If I ever do the book, it will have to treat with the Nazis at least in one section of it. That is why the subject interests me."

"Marta vanished before you arrived to collaborate with her on the book?"

"Yes."

"There was a young man from Berlin here a while ago.

He sort of faded into thin air. I asked Marta about him and she was vague. But I gathered he hadn't turned out as she'd hoped."

"I was told the same thing," she agreed.

"Will you write the book even if Marta doesn't show up?"

"Perhaps. David Leopold thinks I should."

"I'm astonished at that," Rolf said. "I had an idea he would be against it. But you never know."

"Both he and Claude seem to want the book completed," she said. "I may go back to New York with the material and finish it there."

"You'd be much better off here as far as research is concerned," the ski instructor said.

"Perhaps."

"And anyway, I'd like to see you remain here," he said. "We could get to know each other better."

Her eyes met his. "Do you think that would be a good idea?"

"Why not?"

"We might grow to hate each other," she said.

"I'm a very friendly fellow," he protested.

She gave him a studied look. "You appear a very friendly fellow," she said. "I don't think that's the same thing."

"You shock me!" he said. But he didn't sound shocked.

She glanced at her watch and then at the glassed end of the big room. "It's late and dark," she said. "I've stayed longer than I intended."

Rolf Monner smiled at her. "You found the company amusing?"

"I suppose so."

"At least that's a small concession," the ski instructor told her.

She got up and gazed down at the far end of the room. "Where can Gretchen be?"

"Shall we walk down there and take a closer look at the tables for her?"

"Yes. I must get back to the castle."

They moved down the center aisle of the crowded lounge and she searched the faces at every table. There was no sign of Gretchen nor of the young Englishman she'd been with. It was annoying and just about what she might have expected from Gretchen.

She turned to Rolf in alarm. "She's stranded me here. What am I to do?"

"Are you sure?"

"She was sitting at one of these tables. The only other hope is if she's in the lobby."

"Let's find out," the young German said.

They left the music and friendly crowd of the lounge behind and went along the corridor to the lobby. It was not as filled with people as before and it took no more than a moment or two for her to see that Gretchen was not there either.

Rolf said, "We'll see if the station wagon is outside."

She gave him a look of dejection. "I'd almost bet it isn't."

"Let's find out," he said, going ahead and swinging back the big glass door for her.

They went out into the dark and cold and crossed to the parking area. She came to the place where Gretchen had parked the station wagon and the marks of its wheels were there.

"That settles it," she exclaimed. "Can I hire a taxi?"

The tall, blond man said, "There are taxis. But you don't have to hire one. I'll take you to the castle."

"I have no right to impose on you!"

"I'll be glad to do it," he assured her. "My car is over to the side of the lot."

He led her to it and she saw that it was a tiny German car. He opened the door for her and then got behind the wheel himself. He gave her a look of dour amusement. "Like old times when I used to drive Marta back and forth from the castle to the hotel."

She gave him a sharp glance. "You did a lot of that?"

"For a while," he said, as he started the car and began backing out of the lot.

"You were so close to her yet you have no idea where she may be now?"

"No idea at all," he said very definitely as he drove out onto the roadway.

But she did not believe him. There was something in his tone when he said it that suggested he was lying and enjoying the lie. She sat quietly as he drove along the snowy road at a fast speed. Occasionally a car came toward them from the opposite direction, headlights glaring in the dark night.

She wondered where Gretchen could have gone and was angry that her blonde cousin had played such a mean trick on her. It was humiliating to have to depend on the kindness of this comparative stranger to get back to the castle. The afternoon had done little to clear up any of the mystery, though she had enjoyed getting away from the grim atmosphere of the old castle for awhile.

As he drove, Rolf asked, "When do I see you again?"

"Maybe never."

"Was I all that annoying to you?"

"No. But I may return to New York."

"So soon?"

"I haven't made up my mind," she said. "Nothing seems to be happening here. I don't think Marta is ever going to return."

The thin man at the wheel smiled grimly. "Perhaps she'll come back as a ghost and reveal herself to you."

"Enough strange things have happened at the castle already," she said. "I can do without any more."

His eyes were on the road as he said, "Marta always used to rave about how much she liked the castle. It meant all the old days to her. But the last few times we were together she talked in a different way about it."

"What do you mean?"

"It's hard to explain. But she'd taken on a kind of uneasiness. And she seemed almost afraid to go back there."

"Did she tell you she was afraid?"

"Not in so many words, but I sensed it in her."

She was silent a moment. Then she said, "When I was

going through her things today I found an unfinished note. It made a mention of her beginning the year in fear."

He glanced from the wheel to her for a moment. "That supports what I said, doesn't it?"

"It does," she agreed. "If that's what the letter intended to indicate. David Leopold seemed to believe it had something to do with her fear of failure as an actress."

"She knew that fear as well," the German ski instructor said.

"But you believe there was another fear she knew."

"I'd say so."

"Could it have anything to do with her disappearance?"

"It might," he said.

They had reached the castle and he brought the car to a halt before the entrance door. He assisted her out of the car and smiled down at her. Their breaths showed in the cold air.

"I'll be in touch with you later," he promised.

"I may be here," she said.

"Don't leave without telling me," he asked her. And then he took her in his arms and kissed her. "Something to remember me by," he said smilingly.

Before she could offer any rebuke he laughed and hurried back to his car. He waved a final good-bye and she waved in return. It was impossible to be angry with the brash young man. He had a lot of good qualities despite his habit of philandering and his devotion to the Nazis of old.

She opened the heavy oaken door and met Kate Bromley in the reception hall. The big woman looked less than pleased to see her.

She asked, "Kate, is Miss Gretchen at home?"

"Not that I know of, Miss," the Englishwoman said.

"I've a thing or two to say to her," Ina promised.

"I think she went out for the afternoon and hasn't returned yet.

"I know she went out," Ina said bitterly. "I was with her when she left."

The elderly woman showed surprise. "But you came back on your own?"

"She stranded me," she told her. "Left me at the hotel with no way to get here."

"She's quite capable of that," Kate agreed.

"Where is everyone else?"

"Mr. Leopold and Mr. Claude are upstairs in their rooms," she said.

"What is the latest word about Hans?"

The big woman said, "None that I know of. Except those of us on the staff will be given time to attend his funeral. Mr. Leopold was kind enough to grant us that."

"I'm glad," she said.

"Yes, Miss," the other woman said quietly.

"If you see Gretchen before I do, tell her that I'm looking for her, will you?"

"Yes, Miss," the big woman said.

Ina started up the stairs and then halted a few steps on her way. She turned with her hand on the bannister and asked, "Kate, do you think your mistress was afraid of something in the last weeks before she disappeared?"

Kate Bromley's eyes took on a wary look. She said, "What are you talking about, Miss?"

"Did Marta ever show any signs of being afraid of someone or something in this house?"

"I never heard her say anything, Miss."

"Perhaps she showed fear without saying anything?"

"Not that I know of, Miss," Kate Bromley said. "Why do you ask?"

"I heard it mentioned that she was showing signs of fear and I found a note in which she wrote of being afraid of beginning a new year in this house."

Kate showed alarm. "I can't picture Miss Marta writing a thing like that."

"I showed the note to Mr. Leopold," Ina said.

The Englishwoman's face was flushed. She said, "They were all against her here. They did all they could to make her life a misery. And now she's gone!"

With this astonishing declaration the big woman hurried off into the shadows of the main corridor.

Ina gazed after her in amazement. There could be no doubt that Kate Bromley was filled with frustration and resentments. What it all meant was hard to say. The Nazi-loving Englishwoman had been with Marta for many years and undoubtedly hated both Claude and David Leopold for the roles they had played in Marta's life following the war. A mere mention of David Leopold had set off her show of anger.

Now that she had returned to the castle, Ina was more than ever aware of the brooding air which seemed to cloak it. For a short time while she was at the hotel she had relaxed a little. Of course there had been the game of trying to drag out information from Rolf Monner and at the same time not give too many of her own thoughts away. This had been taxing. But at least she had felt free from the eerie atmosphere of suspense which she continually experienced in the old castle.

She reached the first landing and then climbed the stairs to the second and finally the third on which her own room was located. It seemed more shadowed and menacing than any of the others but she tried to make herself believe that this was purely her imagination.

Many phantoms walked in these corridors. The history of the castle was bound to go back a century or more. And in the time in which it had been occupied by Marta Landen many had come and gone. No wonder that Marta might have had apprehensions about beginning another year under its roof. So many of those she'd known had faded into the past, dim ghosts almost forgotten.

Of course the name of Karl Bruck lived on because of his infamy. And she was not at all sure but that the Nazi did haunt the place. She had known several strange experiences since her arrival and all had hinted of the supernatural. Even her uncle's death had been of a suspicious nature. Had he died of a heart seizure or had someone decided to eliminate him to prevent him producing his play depicting the Nazis as villains?

If there had been foul play in her uncle's death it had been cleverly concealed. But surely Marta must have known all that was going on. And now she had vanished! With these tormenting thoughts Ina opened the door of her room and turned on the lights. She made her way over to the dresser mirror to study herself a moment and felt that she looked exhausted.

She was still staring in the mirror when she saw a terribly scarred and mutilated face reflected there. Long hair straggled down to the shoulders of the macabre creature as the face showed itself in the mirror over her right shoulder. She screamed.

CHAPTER NINE

The scream seemed to act like a cue for the face to vanish. For vanish it did! She wheeled around and saw she was alone in the room. One of the closets was open and it struck her the phantom might have vanished in there but she could not be sure. Still trembling from fright, she slowly advanced to the closet and glanced into its shadows.

She touched a switch and the walk-in closet was now flooded with light. Her clothes hung there undisturbed and there was no sign of an intruder lurking. It made her question her senses. Surely she had seen someone. Or was it a trick of her imagination?

She doubted this since it was exactly the same disfigured face she'd seen before and which had stalked her in the corridor. Was it a ghost she'd seen—the features of some unfortunate who had lived and died in the old castle? She forced herself to begin changing for the evening though she was still in a feverish state of nerves.

Nothing else happened to upset her and a half-hour later she went back down the stairs. As she reached the lower level of the castle she heard Claude playing in the music room. He was part way through a bright Gypsy air and giving it the touch of a master. She knew the wild, abandoned music but she felt she had never heard it played to such advantage before. She stood enthralled outside the door of the music room until he played the final bars of the piece and put his violin down.

Then she advanced into the room and applauded him. "That was a treat," she said.

His handsome face flushed with pleasure. "It's a simple selection but one I enjoy."

She looked up at him with admiring eyes. "You have a magic touch."

"Long hours of practice," he told her.

"And great talent," she insisted. "Don't deny it. Marta must have taken great pleasure in your music."

At the mention of his mother's name his face became solemn. "I miss playing for her," he admitted. "She had a number of favorite pieces she had me play every time I returned home."

"When do you have to resume your touring?" she asked.

He sighed. "Fairly soon. I don't know what to do. I hate to leave with things as they are. And yet I have my career to look after."

"Surely the police have had time now to locate your mother if she is still alive," she argued.

Claude Leopold looked troubled. "The police claim that often in these amnesia cases the missing person actually assumes a very different identity. They look and act differently from their normal selves and this makes it hard to trace them."

"You still feel that she lost her memory and wandered off?"

"It's the most hopeful theory," he said.

"Is that why you cling to it?"

He stared at her. "Are you saying that I'm not being realistic?"

"Perhaps I am," she admitted.

"What other explanation could there be?"

"She might have left for some reason unknown to you. Or she might have gone out to meet someone only to be murdered and her body hidden by someone else."

"I can't picture that happening," he protested.

"I can," she said.

He stared at her. "You're serious?"

"Yes."

"Then you must be aware of things here which are hidden from me," the young man said.

She looked at him gravely. "Only tonight I had another strange experience."

"What sort of experience?"

"You remember I told you I saw a face in the shadows of the corridor? A terribly mutilated man's face?"

Claude frowned. "I seem to remember vaguely."

"I saw that face again tonight. Staring over my shoulder into the mirror!"

"Then what?"

"I screamed and turned to get a better look at whoever it was, but in that short second he had vanished."

The young violinist looked at her incredulously. "If he had ever been there at all!"

"I tell you I saw the face," she insisted.

"Wouldn't it be nearer the truth to say that you remembered the face and your mind formed a picture of it?"

"It was a reflection in my mirror! The reflection of a horrible face!"

He shrugged. "What can I say? You see faces that vanish and are stalked by phantoms which disappear before anyone arrives to help you. Couldn't you just be suffering from a bad case of nerves?"

"No."

"So we come to the usual impasse," he said. "Where were you all afternoon?"

"At the hotel," she said. "Gretchen invited me to go to the afternoon tea dance with her."

Claude looked slightly displeased. "Oh?"

"Yes. I foolishly agreed to go. And when we arrived she ran off with some young Englishman and left me alone."

"That sounds like Gretchen," he said.

"That wasn't the worst of it. She stranded me there."

"How did you get back?"

"I met Rolf Monner again. It was his day off. He

brought me a drink and we danced. Then when he found I had no transportation he brought me here."

Claude looked cynical. "I told you that you'd hear from him again."

"It wasn't anything," she said. "I find him amusing."

"There is another side to him not so pleasant," the young musician reminded her in a dry voice.

"As far as I'm concerned he was all right."

"He'll be phoning you soon. I predict it."

"I won't be available. It was Gretchen who left me there at his mercy."

Claude said, "That might have been deliberate."

She was surprised. "You think so?"

"Who knows?"

"Why would she do that?"

"Aren't she and Rolf pretty close?"

She shook her head. "Not any longer. They had a quarrel because Rolf was also paying attention to your mother."

He looked grim. "I know about that."

"So they aren't speaking now. They avoid each other."

"That's a good story anyhow," he said.

She stared at him. "You don't believe it?"

"Let's say I'm not completely convinced," Claude said. "And Gretchen isn't back yet?"

"I guess not."

"One of these days my sister is going to get herself in serious trouble," he predicted. "That is if she hasn't done it already."

"I still can't make up my mind about her," Ina admitted.

"I can," Claude said. "She's not to be trusted in any way."

"That's very harsh."

"It also happens to be true."

"Yet I'm sure she's badly upset about what happened to her mother. Even though they didn't get on."

"She'd want us to believe that anyway," he said with a look of disgust.

"Where would Gretchen go with that Englishman?" she wondered.

"They've probably stopped some place in the village for dinner," he said. "There are dozens of good little places."

"I wish I was with her," she said with a tiny shudder. "I'm beginning to find this house very oppressive."

"Do you plan to stay and work on the book?"

"Maybe."

"You haven't decided yet?"

"Not completely."

"My father told me that you had."

"He may have taken that from something I said, but I have never made a definite promise."

Claude said, "Why are you having such a difficult job deciding about it?"

"Perhaps because of the atmosphere here. I find the castle full of strange hatreds and macabre influences," she said. "I don't know whether I can work well under those circumstances."

"It shouldn't be too hard. And you're almost bound to get a best seller out of it. Mother was an exciting personality in her prime."

"I'd find it so much easier if she were here to check on me and make sure I had the facts correctly, that the dates were right and all the rest. But instead she's still missing."

"And liable to be," Claude said soberly.

"I think only your father really expects her to return to us alive."

Claude gave her a meaningful look. "Yet he has given you permission to sift through her papers."

"That means he does have doubts."

The young violinist gave her a look of rueful amusement. "If Mother should return and discover you intruded on her privacy, don't expect to get off lightly."

"That worries me a little."

"It should. She can be vindictive."

"I tried to query Kate Bromley about her tonight and she became very upset."

155

He frowned. "Kate is so devoted to Mother. And Hans' death hasn't been easy on her."

"It must have upset all the servants."

"Things are very unsettled backstairs. Father says that Mrs. Horst is trying to take over but it won't be easy."

"Rolf said that Hans had a son in the German army."

"Rolf's father also served Hitler," Claude said. "Did he tell you how proud that made him feel?"

"He said the equivalent of that."

The young violinist looked disgusted. "I'd like to throttle him every time he says it."

"I have an idea it is said mostly for effect. He's had good results saying it other times. So he keeps it up. The wicked young rebel image, you know."

"I know him too well," Claude said with disgust. "While you were wasting your time with him you had a phone call."

"From who?"

He smiled thinly. "No one you know well. Otto Fess called. He says that his wife is very anxious to talk to you. He wanted to know if you'd stop by their place tonight."

"What did you tell him?"

"I was in a spot," Claude said. "I didn't know where you were. So I simply said that you'd go visit Pauline this evening if you had nothing else arranged."

"I'd like to see her," she said. "How will I get there?"

"I imagine Otto would send his chauffeur here to pick you up. But if you like I'll go over with you and use my station wagon."

She smiled. "That would make it more pleasant."

"Then consider it arranged," he said. "I promised to meet Father in the drawing room for a drink. He'll be wondering what happened to me."

He and Ina moved on to the drawing room to discover the elderly David Leopold standing before the full-length portrait of Marta Landen with his drink in his hand. When he heard them coming in he turned to them with a slightly startled look.

He said, "You must forgive an old man's whim. Being

alone in this big room made me realize how much I missed Marta. In a moment I found myself staring up at her portrait like any immature young fan."

Claude smiled sympathetically. "That's the effect she has always had on people. Call it glamour, charm or whatever you like, Mother had what it required to be a star." And turning to Ina he said, "I'll get us drinks and bring them back here." And he moved on to the bar.

Left alone with the gray-haired man she said, "I know just how you must feel. This big portrait exerts a kind of spell over me and I scarcely knew her."

David Leopold pointed a stubby forefinger at the portrait. "That is what she was like when I first met her! And she was just as beautiful that last night of the party on New Year's Eve. Poor old Hans! I recall him peeking at her from around the corner of the hallway when things were under way. He had a great love for Marta. And now he is gone!"

"It is very sad."

The old man had a far-away look in his eyes as he went on, "Marta could be as difficult as she was beautiful," he said. "I have often had people ask me how I could put up with her. They didn't understand how much I loved this woman. When there is love there is no sacrifice which is too demanding. I loved Marta."

"I'm sure you did," she said.

He turned to the portrait again. "I came here after the war, closer to being dead than alive. I had given up all hope of living and even of life itself. I wanted to die! Marta made me want to live again!"

Ina stared at him. "Then you knew Marta before. I mean before you were placed in that concentration camp."

The thick-set old man nodded. "Yes. I was a theatre manager in Munich. It wasn't a very important theatre but I had charge of it. Marta played there several times and over the years we became friends."

"Then you were separated by the war?"

"That is correct," David Leopold said. "But Marta somehow learned where I was. When she heard I was among the living she asked that I come here. Her husband had just been drowned and she told me she needed someone to stand by her—someone strong, and she asked that it be I. I who was almost too weak to stand on my own two feet. It was charity but charity of such a splendid sort that one could not refuse."

"I'm sure she was sincere."

"I must believe that," the old man said. "And after we were married I suggested that we have a son. And she told me we would have. A son from the same death camps which had so nearly claimed me. And that was when we adopted Claude."

Claude came back with the drinks and with a smile asked his father, "Did I hear my name mentioned?"

"You did," David Leopold said. "I was once again telling Miss Sperling the story of our lives. I expect I have bored her."

Ina shook her head. "No. I think it is a wonderful story. It bears repeating. I only wish that it had a happier ending. That she were here to join us!"

The old man stared at the smiling portrait and sighed, "Will that ever be?"

They went in to dinner and David Leopold complained that Gretchen had not returned. Ina tried to make excuses for her spirited cousin but she could tell the old man was badly worried. Later, when Claude told his father they were also going out to visit the Fesses, he seemed quite upset. The mysterious death of Hans seemed to have shaken him more than they'd guessed.

The old man looked at them and said, "Then I shall be left here alone?"

Claude said, "Unless you wish to come along?"

David Leopold scowled. "And be at the mercy of Pauline Fess and her fantasies all evening. No thanks. Marta could bear with her, but I've not got her patience."

Ina said, "I'm sorry to leave you alone. But we did promise to make the visit."

"Go ahead," the old man said. "I'll smoke a good cigar and go to bed."

So they left the house around nine in the station wagon. There was still no sign of Gretchen or her car. It was all too likely, Claude speculated, that she was carousing on the town.

"There are pre-Lenten parties everywhere," he told Ina. "And no doubt Gretchen and her friend have found one. If that's the case don't look for them until very late indeed."

Sitting beside him in the semi-darkness of the wagon's front seat, she said, "Your father seemed very much on edge, didn't he?"

Claude's handsome profile registered worry. "I think Hans being found dead and perhaps murdered has frightened him. He is beginning to lose hope of seeing Mother alive again."

"Rolf Monner claims we never will see her."

Claude glanced away from the road a moment. "Perhaps he knows more than we do."

Her eyes were frightened. "You shouldn't say such things without some proof."

"I'm very suspicious of Rolf," he said. "And I'm still not making any bets that he isn't working along with Gretchen."

"They're not even speaking!"

That might be a convenient pretence for them," was the young man's reply.

"You think so? You're going on the theory that Gretchen and her mother never did get over that major quarrel they had. And that Gretchen arranged her murder for revenge."

"I'd say it was possible and that Rolf, in an attempt to get himself in Gretchen's good graces once more, helped. Naturally they would go on with a charade of being at odds. It would be their best alibi."

"How can you offer such a possibility so casually?" she exclaimed. "The very idea makes my blood run cold."

"It's a classic situation. You should read more Greek drama," he told her. "On the other hand, if I found it out to be true I'd probably be sick to my stomach."

"I'm glad," she said. "At least it proves that you're human."

"All too human and open to error," the young man said. "I hope this errand tonight is not one of them."

"What can Pauline Fess have to say to me?" she wondered.

"That's what I'm asking myself."

"Probably it's about the book. She was in the theatre with Marta and she'll be hoping to be included in it in a very good light."

He said, "There is one other possibility."

"What?"

"It may be Otto who is worried."

She stared at him. "About what?"

"His past."

"So he has one too!"

"Indeed. One of the most valued of Hitler's commanders, I understand," Claude said as he brought the car to a halt.

She said, "It looks just like where you live only it is a good deal smaller."

"It was built about the same time," he agreed, "and much of the plan is identical."

She hesitated before getting out of the car. "What were you going to tell me about Otto Fess?"

"He was one of those questioned about atrocities in the field after the war," Claude said. "Can you imagine his straight-backed reaction to that? In the end they couldn't decide on his guilt and so he was released."

"But you think it was a near thing with him?"

Claude smiled bitterly. "I think he was guilty and lucky enough to get off. But then don't take my word for it. I'm prejudiced."

"What else do you know about him?" she asked.

"Well, he was one of those close to Karl Bruck, and you know the sort he was."

"Everyone seems to think him the embodiment of evil," she said.

"A person of a double nature. On the one hand he was

a lover of music, a devoted opera fan, a dear friend of my mother's, and in contrast he was an ardent Nazi, a genius at cruelty and a perpetrator of great evils."

Ina said, "He must have had a forceful personality or the local people would not still remember him and think that they see his ghost."

"They're still frightened of him," David said. "And he's been dead almost longer than I've lived."

She glanced toward the gray castle, mantled in snow with amber lights showing at several of its arched windows. "And Otto was one of his cronies."

"Just remember that. No matter how coldly polite Otto may be to us this evening, don't forget that he was one of them."

"I won't. No wonder that Pauline has become a little strange. Living with that sort of evil can't be easy."

"I agree," he said. "Well, shall we make our entrance?"

"I suppose we should," she said.

They got out of the wagon and crossed the snow to the steps. Claude rang the entrance bell and they waited for a moment. Then the door was opened by Otto Fess himself, wearing an expensive smoking jacket.

He bowed in military fashion, from the hips and with a tense movement. "Delighted that you could come, Miss Sperling. And you as well, Claude." There was less warmth in his greeting to Claude, she noted.

Claude said, "We're happy to be able to come."

As the stiff-backed Prussian led them into the reception hall, he said, "You may not have heard but we are going to hold a costume ball here the night before Lent. I know it was Marta's project, but with her missing there was some concern that the event might not be held. So my wife and I have agreed to offer the use of our home for it."

Claude looked serious. "Even if my mother should return I doubt that she'd be in any fit state of mind to take the responsibility for such an important social event."

Otto Fess explained to her, "It is the final of the *Fasching* events. Something like your Mardi Gras in New Orleans. The whole village will be celebrating and there will be many costume parties. I plan only to invite the group we've had over the years plus a few newcomers."

"It sounds very exciting," Ina agreed.

The thin man with the scar running down his cheek smiled sourly. "We have never held the party here before. It was always at Marta's. But under the circumstances people were beginning to worry. At least this way we're sure there will be a party." He turned to Claude again. "Any further word about your mother?"

"Nothing. And now the police are busy investigating the circumstances surrounding Hans' death."

Otto Fess lifted his eyebrows. "I understood his death was the result of an accident."

"They must be sure," Claude told him. "So they will go on asking questions and making tests."

"As a military man may I say the fallacy is they never seem to satisfactorily close a case," Otto Fess said.

"I know exactly what you mean," Claude admitted. "I wish we were either on the German or Swiss side. I'm sure then we'd get better action from the authorities."

"It could not be worse," was the older man's opinion. He turned to Ina again and said, "It appears that you made a strong impression on my wife when she met you at the castle."

"I'm pleased," she said.

"You should be," Otto Fess said, his cold eyes fixed on her. "She wants to see you because she has been having some very strange dreams lately."

"I see," Ina ventured, hardly knowing what to say.

"My wife is somewhat odd," Fess said with some awkwardness. "I am worried about a repeated dream she has been having. I hoped seeing you might get it off her mind."

"I'll be only too happy to do anything I can," she said as the three of them stood in the shadows of the hallway at the foot of the stairs.

"Well, now I've told you the crux of my problem," Otto Fess said arrogantly.

Claude said, "It is natural she should miss my mother. They were such good friends."

"Yes," Otto Fess said with a frown. "And there are other fancies she indulges in which disturb me. She is a good deal older than Marta was. When they acted together she was playing the roles of older women when Marta was a girl."

"So I've been told," she said.

Otto Fess showed interest on his gaunt face as he asked her, "You are delving into the material which Marta gathered about her life and career?"

"Yes," she said, "I am. I've just started."

Those cold eyes bored into her. "You will find much of interest. No doubt there will be references to my wife."

"I would expect so," she agreed. "She should certainly be in the book."

"And myself?" Otto Fess asked. "What about me?"

She said, "I haven't gotten back that far as yet. But I have been told the notes are very complete."

"Then they will mention Karl Bruck? Fess snapped the words.

"Yes," she said, a little shocked by his tense manner. "I believe he was a friend of Marta's."

"He was her great friend, the man in her life," the gaunt man said sternly. "And he was also a friend of mine and of Pauline's. No book would be complete without a good bit in it about Bruck."

Claude had been standing quietly in the shadowed lower hall as they all talked. His handsome face now rather pale, he questioned Otto Fess: "Do you expect Karl Bruck to be treated in a heroic manner in the book? If so, I doubt if Marta would approve."

The former army officer glared at the young man. "Why should she not approve?"

"My mother went to great lengths to correct the widespread belief that she was a Nazi sympathizer."

Otto Fess eyed him bleakly. "It is of no importance to me what Marta did or her motives for doing so. Your foster mother was very anxious about her career after Germany was defeated. I think her actions then reflected her needs rather than her beliefs."

Claude's lip curled slightly. "You are suggesting that her marriage and her adoption of me were purely moves to take the smear from her reputation?"

"I prefer not to think about it," the grizzled Otto Fess said coldly. "We were all plunged into a world in which survival was the prime thing. Now if you would like to go up and see my wife?"

"Yes, that would be very nice," Ina said quickly, afraid that the bitter words between the two men might lead to some other exchange.

Otto Fess started up the stairway, "We have located our drawing room on the second floor in the manner of many European homes. And our ballroom is located on the third floor. That is where we shall be holding the *Faschingsdienstag*."

"I hope I shall still be here," she said as she went up the stairs beside him, Claude following in the rear.

He glanced at her. "You are thinking of leaving?"

"It depends on whether Marta returns or not."

"Poor Marta!" Fess said with a sigh. "And now Hans is dead! The castle will not be the same!"

They reached the landing and went through a double doorway to the drawing room. It was a high-ceilinged room with great shimmering chandeliers and crowded with elegant period furniture. Tapestries and fine paintings hung from the walls and a thick Oriental rug covered its floor.

On a divan by a marble fireplace with a flaming log fire sat the aged Pauline Fess, her fingers working busily at an embroidery project. As they entered the room she raised her eyes to give them a pale smile of greeting.

The regal old woman put down her embroidery and advanced across the room to meet them. "How good you are to cater to an old woman's whim and visit me!" she exclaimed. And she kissed Ina on the cheek. Then she shook hands with Claude.

Otto Fess said, "Come, let us all make ourselves comfortable by the fire. It is a cold night."

"This house is hard to heat," Pauline Fess said. "We need the fireplaces lighted all over the house."

Ina gazed around her. "It's a lovely place."

"Not as large as the castle," Otto Fess said. "But plenty of room for two old people."

His wife smiled vaguely. "One hardly realizes it, that one is old. But it is true." She turned to Ina. "Let me show you the portrait of Marta before we sit down. You as well, Claude."

She led them to the other end of the room to a head and shoulders portrait of Marta in dark tones in a gold frame. It was a young, defiant Marta with a smile of mischief.

"Wasn't she lovely?" Pauline Fess said, staring at the painting with her faded blue eyes.

"It's the study of Mother I like best," Claude agreed. "The one at the castle is imposing but too large. This gives you all the magic of her charm."

Ina agreed. "I like the one at the castle but I think this is better."

Otto Fess was standing by them. He said, "The artist who did that was one of Berlin's best. We have another by him. It is over on the opposite wall." And he led them across the room to another portrait of the same size in an elaborate frame.

When Ina saw this portrait she was convinced that Otto Fess had deliberately drawn their attention to it to annoy Claude. It was a study of a youngish man in an SS officer's uniform. The face had no particular character but the eyes had a chilling coldness to them and the man wore a monocle in one eye. It had to be a painting of Karl Bruck!

Ina said, "You can tell it is the work of the same artist."

Otto Fess had a smug look on his gaunt face. "It was done about the same time."

Claude said nothing but moved away toward the fireplace. In a moment they all went down to that end of the room. Ina sat by Pauline Fess who picked up her embroidery again. Claude sat in a chair opposite them while Otto Fess stood by the fireplace with a look of annoyance on his scarred face.

He asked his wife, "Must you do that endless embroidery while we are entertaining guests?"

"I'm sure they won't mind, my dear," she said. And she turned to Ina, "Do you?"

"No," she replied.

"Still," Otto Fess persisted, "I say it is not polite!"

"Very well," his wife said with a sigh and put the embroidery down beside her. She turned to Ina. "What a tragedy about poor Hans!"

"Yes," Ina said. "I didn't know him well but he was a great favorite at the castle."

"I'm sure of that," Pauline Fess said. "He was struck down on one of the snow-covered hills. Beaten to death so I hear."

Claude said, "The police haven't decided about that. They think some careless skier may have run into him and caused his injuries that way. He was old and not agile. He would not be able to move quickly to save himself."

Otto Fess seemed to be considering this. He said, "Then they don't think it was a murder?"

"They're not sure," Claude said.

Ina addressed the former army officer. "One of the strange things is that when they found him he had a medal in his hand. An iron cross!"

Otto Fess eyed her sternly. "Are you sure of that?"

Claude spoke up. "It's true. I saw the medal."

"Where is it now?" their host wanted to know. His tone was strangely agitated.

Claude said, "The police have it. It seemed it might indicate some clue to the identity of whoever it was ran him down."

Ina said, "Some claim that he had the medal in his hand before he went out of the house. He had a son in the army and the medal may have been his."

"Yes," Otto Fess said stiffly, "he had a son killed in defence of the Fatherland. I know all about that."

Pauline spoke up in her nervous fashion, "I suppose the locals will blame his death on the Satan of the Slopes!"

Otto gave her a look of reprimand. "Please!"

She looked at him innocently. "Really, my dear, there is no secret about it. I'm sure these two young people have heard the legend." She turned to Ina to explain. "You see in the old days when Karl Bruck came here to holiday and ski the locals called him the Satan of the Slopes! They never liked the Nazis here. We were only tolerated."

"They are not interested," Otto Fess protested, obviously upset at his wife's revelations.

"I only wanted to let them understand," she said. "Now they say that the ghost of Karl Bruck returns to ski down the slopes on certain nights. So now it is the ghost of the Satan of the Slopes! And of course they'll claim the ghost killed Hans. But Karl would never do that. Not even as a ghost. Hans was his trusted servant! There was only one person Karl cared more about and that was Marta!"

The grizzled old Otto Fess was glowering at his wife in a most menacing fashion. He said, "Surely you have rambled on long enough. These young people aren't interested in your ghost stories!"

"But this has all to do with the present as well," the pale old woman said. "I'm sure that it was Karl who returned and spirited Marta away. And now Marta is also a ghost!"

Claude frowned and leaned forward to ask the strange old woman, "Why do you say my mother is a ghost? Do you think she is dead?"

"But she must be!" Pauline Fess said. "She comes to my room every night. I see her standing at the foot of my bed. And she is as lovely as ever but quite transparent. You can see right through her! Poor dear Marta!"

CHAPTER TEN

There was a long moment of tense, embarrassed silence in the room on the heels of the strange old woman's amazing statement. At the fireplace Otto Fess looked as if he would like to strike his wife. Claude sat back in his chair looking wan and upset. Ina tried to think of something to say to the slightly mad Pauline.

Strangely it was the old woman herself who broke the taut atmosphere. With a look of uneasiness and a twisting of her frail, heavily veined hands, she said, "I suppose you think that I am quite mad. But it is not so. I have always had a kind of second-sight. I am known to be receptive to spirits."

Her husband said sternly, "We will accept that, Pauline, if you will say no more on the subject."

She looked up at him piteously. "But I have seen Marta's ghost and I see no reason why I shouldn't mention it."

"Claude is your guest," Otto Fess said, "it cannot be pleasant for him to hear you talking about his mother's ghost. Especially since no one can be sure that she is dead."

"She is surely dead," Pauline Fess insisted. "Otherwise why should her ghost come to me?"

Claude spoke up, "I understand, Pauline. We know how close you were to Mother. Naturally you've been worried about her. And your worry is reflected in this reaction."

Ina thought it was a marvel of evasion on the young violinist's part. He was telling the old woman she was having fancies due to her grief but he was making it seem that this was quite understandable, so her feelings would not be hurt.

The elderly actress responded to his words with a wavering smile on her thin lips. "You are right, Claude. But then you always were a sensitive boy and a credit to poor dear Marta."

"Thank you," Claude said solemnly.

Otto Fess looked relieved and almost grateful to Claude. He turned to him, saying, "How much longer will you remain in St. Anton? I know you do not have too much time between tours."

Claude said, "I was scheduled to leave next week. But if Mother does not return I doubt if I'll leave. I shall have to try and have some other artist fill in my bookings."

Otto turned to her. "And you, Miss Sperling?"

"My plans are much like Claude's," she said. "It all depends on whether Marta returns."

"In that case you should both be here for my party," Otto Fess said. "And I shall try and coax David to come as well. He needs to have time away from the castle. He is too depressed by all that has happened there."

"I agree," Claude said. "But he is old and hard to reason with."

"I know best how to handle him," Otto Fess said.

Pauline rose nervously and said to Ina, "May I show you my room and some of the rest of the house?"

"I'd enjoy that," Ina said, rising.

"Then I'm sure the gentlemen will excuse us," the old actress said with an arch smile.

Otto Fess looked slightly distressed. "Do you feel this is necessary, Pauline?"

"I do," she said brightly. "As our guest this young woman has a right to be shown around."

"Very well," her husband said, looking defeated. His straight, lean body was outlined against the glow from the fireplace.

Pauline Fess led Ina from room to room, talking vaguely all the while. Some of her comments made good sense while others were strange and disjointed. When they arrived at a small, neat room with print curtains in the back of the house, the old woman sighed.

"This is my sewing room. Marta and I used to sit here and sew and talk. You wouldn't think that a glamorous creature like her would be interested in sewing. But she was. It dated back to her early days in the theatre."

"I suppose she had to make her own dresses then to save money," Ina suggested.

"She did. And she learned to do it well. As we became older and had time on our hands here, we both returned to sewing again. Marta came over here whenever she had a chance and we would talk about the good old days. And just before she vanished she came and stayed all one afternoon and left her sewing basket behind for when she'd return again. But she never will return again."

Since they were by themselves in the isolated room, Ina felt she could tackle the subject directly. She said, "Why are you convinced that Marta is dead?"

"I know she has been murdered."

"How can you know?"

The old woman's smile was madly reasonable. "Because I have seen her ghost. Didn't I tell you?"

"Is that your sole basis for your belief?" she persisted.

The elderly woman hesitated a moment and then leaned forward to her confidentially. "No," she said, in a low voice, close to a whisper. "No. There was something else."

"What?"

"Marta was frightened!"

Ina felt her heart leap. It brought back the message of the unfinished note in which Marta had written of beginning the New Year in fear.

She said, "Frightened?"

"Yes."

"Of what?"

"Of life," the old woman said with a crafty look on her

lined face. "Marta knew her time had passed. She didn't want to be forgotten. It was very hard for her."

"But who was she frightened of?"

Pauline Fess hesitated. "I'm not sure. Maybe of Karl. You see, she had married twice since his death. And that last marriage would never have pleased Karl. I think she was terrified he would reach out from the grave to seek vengeance."

"You really believe that?"

"Oh, yes. I think so. And that is what must have happened in the end. Karl Bruck came and whisked her off to the land of the dead with him. Now he has her again."

Ina stared at the old woman, not knowing whether she was playing a droll game on her or whether this was what she actually believed. With Pauline it was hard to tell.

She said, "What now?"

"Nothing," the old woman said. "Everything should be at rest. Karl and Marta are no longer parted. If only we could all return to the old days as easily."

Ina said, "You think only of the past. Marta lived for the present."

Pauline Fess shook her head. "Marta was only a phantom in these painful times. All that she had loved, the people she loved, had been lost."

"And now Hans has been killed," Ina said.

The pale blue eyes of the old woman fixed on her. "You know why he had to die?"

"No."

"Because he was faithful to Marta. He would want to protect her. Try to save her from being transported to the other side."

"You're saying that Hans was killed by the ghost of Karl Bruck because he wanted to save her from him?"

"It had to be that," Pauline Fess said solemnly. "Otherwise Karl would never have struck down Hans. It was only because the old man resented his taking her from this world!"

"You have a strange explanation for it all," Ina said.

"You mustn't tell my husband anything I've said to

you," the old woman went on. "He doesn't understand. He thinks I'm mad. And you know I'm really much more intelligent than he is. I always was."

She was forced to smile at the old actress in her seriousness. She said, "I'll keep silent on all you've told me. You may count on me."

"You are a good girl," Pauline said. "Not like that other one. That Gretchen is a vixen!"

"She and Marta didn't get on."

"Of course not!" Pauline exclaimed with a spirit surprising in one as frail as she seemed to be. "What mother could bear with a daughter like that? Gretchen will come to no good end! Mark my words!"

"I hope you are wrong," she said. "But she is spoiled and wayward."

"Vixen!" Pauline declared as she led Ina back to the drawing room and the others.

Claude and Otto were standing before the fireplace with glasses in their hands talking quietly when Ina and the old woman came back into the room.

Pauline Fess went directly to her husband and said, "Otto, we mustn't!"

He stared at her with a surprised expression on his gaunt, scarred face. "Mustn't what?"

"Mustn't have that vixen to our party!" his wife declared.

His eyebrow's lifted. "I fear I don't know what you're trying to tell me. What vixen?"

"That Gretchen! I don't want her to be invited for the costume ball!" the old woman protested.

Otto Fess looked relieved. "Is that all? Well, I'm afraid we can't do anything about that. An invitation had already been sent to both Gretchen and her father. It was the only kind thing to do with her mother missing."

"Gretchen hated her mother!" his wife said.

"Still, we can be tolerant," Otto said placatingly. And to Ina he said, "I trust you enjoyed your tour of the house."

"Very much," she said.

Claude gave her a meaningful glance. "Don't you think

we should start back? It's getting late and it is very cold."

"Yes, we should," she said, taking up the cue.

Otto Fess said, "There is no need to hurry." But he sounded as if he wouldn't mind if they left.

His wife said, "You must come again. We get so lonely here."

"I will," Ina promised.

They said their good nights to the old actress and then Otto Fess led them back downstairs to get their things from the closet. As he helped Ina into her coat, he said, "I hope you will forgive my wife."

Ina said, "She is a very interesting person."

There was a grim look on his gaunt face. He said, "She is a little mad. One must frankly face it."

She said, "Perhaps peculiar would be a fairer term."

"I cannot gloss over her insanity," Otto Fess said. "I have to live with it every day. But fortunately she is still able to enjoy most things."

"She is rather sweet and very well-intentioned," Ina said.

"I'm glad you feel that way about her," he said sternly. "You must visit us again and you both must come to our party."

They exchanged good nights and were on their way. In the station wagon Claude gave a great sigh. "That was some ordeal, wasn't it?"

She smiled at him grimly. "You didn't exactly hit it off too well with our host," she said.

At the wheel Claude said, "I dislike Nazis on sight. And he was one of them. You can smell it. So was she but not so dangerous. He could have killed her for giving them away."

"But surely you have always known they were Hitlerites."

"They've never admitted it before. And she was the one to do it today. Otto was properly outraged."

"For them the good world died with Hitler and the defeat of Germany."

"No question about that," he said, his eyes on the road

ahead. "Now they try to behave like respectable citizens."

"They are respectable citizens today. What can you do?"

Claude said, "Wish that they had been punished for their evil."

"Not Pauline. She is just a poor old woman who happened to have been mixed up with that crowd."

"I'll agree she is harmless enough today. But how many do you suppose she betrayed in that long-ago era?"

"Probably none. I don't see Pauline as political."

He said, "You two were gone long enough. What did she have to say?"

"Just a lot of talk about Marta. She was so dedicated to her. She really believes Marta was the victim of Karl Bruck's avenging ghost."

"That's pretty," he said bitterly.

"I know, but she has it in her mind and you can't change her. That's why she imagines she sees Marta's ghost."

"And they're going to have the Mardi Gras party," Claude said with disgust. "They'll be bound to get a crowd. People will flock anywhere they can be entertained with food and drink for free."

"That's true. He's probably inviting everyone and he'll get most of the old crowd and a lot of new fringe people as well."

"It's his money. I suppose he has a right to do as he likes with it."

"Perhaps."

He looked at her from the wheel. You don't sound as if you believed it."

"It's all a strange business," Ina said. "Most of these people are wrapped up in their dreams of the past. Living on them. Marta wasn't as bad as many of them, but she must have suffered from the same illness to a degree."

"Probably she did. I didn't notice it," he admitted. "Like all the rest I was taken in by her charm. I thought she loved me!" "I'm sure she did," Ina said quietly. "She was very proud of your music."

Claude's handsome face showed his grief. "Or was it

that she was delighted with having David and me as token Jews?"

"It could have even started with that," Ina said. "But in the end I'm certain she came to truly care for you both."

"Now that's a very delightful picture you paint," he said, "but I'm not sure I believe it."

"I want you to," she said earnestly. "I can't bear to see you made unhappy."

"Thanks."

"I mean it."

He said, "What did you make of the portrait of Karl Bruck?"

"I don't know," she said. "There's a strange elusiveness about him. As if he were a sort of chameleon. He shows no distinctive character in the portrait. There was just one thing."

"What?"

"His eyes. He had penetrating, cruel eyes. And oddly they seemed to remind me of someone."

At the wheel Claude frowned. "To be truthful I had the same feeling. I wonder where I've seen those eyes."

"Never. He was dead before you were born or about the time of your birth."

"Still those eyes haunt me," he said, then he seemed to suddenly be reminded of something. "I know where I've seen them."

"Where?" she asked.

"I'd better not say! You'll make too much of it."

"You fascinate me," she said to the young man at the wheel as they drove along the snow-lined road, the beam of their headlights glowing against the darkness of the night. "You'll have to tell me now."

"His eyes remind me of Rolf Monner's," he said.

"But Rolf is no older than you are. So he could have had nothing to do with Karl Bruck."

"Just a minute," Claude said excitedly. "Isn't he always saying how proud he is of being a German?"

"That's not a crime or even wrong."

"He means he's proud that he is a descendant of the

Germans who were going to rule the world. The storm troopers who were so sure that tomorrow belonged to them!"

"So?"

"How do we know his name is Monner?"

"We don't, I suppose."

"Why couldn't it be Bruck? Karl Bruck's son."

"As far as the records go Bruck wasn't married, was he?" she asked.

"Who could keep records on those Nazis? Bruck was supposed to be my mother's lover, but it is two chances to one that he had a wife hidden away somewhere. Maybe a woman he deserted."

"I suppose it could be," she said.

"I'll bet he is Bruck's son. That's why he came here to the countryside his father loved. So the Satan of the Slopes does ski down them again!"

"You said I'd make too much of it," she warned him. "And now you are. Even if Rolf has the same sort of eyes we saw in that portrait, you can't rush off and invent a whole fictional relationship between the two to explain it. Lots of people who are in no way related have the same sort of eyes."

"Still we may have hit on something in this," Claude insisted as he speeded up the car again.

"I doubt it."

"Suppose Rolf came here to avenge his father! And he charmed Gretchen and Marta, setting them against each other! And then he killed Marta. And probably Hans, because he knew Bruck had a son and suspected him!"

"Too melodramatic!"

"I say no! I say Rolf will bear watching. And I'll also try to find out if his name is truly Monner."

"You may be wasting your time," she warned him.

"I'll talk to the police. They've done little or nothing about mother's disappearance. It's time they showed some interest. They can at least investigate Rolf's background."

She sighed. "I'm afraid you're too worked up about this."

"But it's all so logical."

"You make it *seem* logical," she corrected him.

"Well, anyway, you know what I mean!"

"Poor Claude!" she said, snuggling close to him.

"Don't pity me!" he said. "I don't want that!"

She smiled ruefully up at him, her head nestled on his shoulder. "I'm in love with you. It has nothing to do with pity. Nothing at all."

He glanced at her only half-convinced. "Sure?"

"Yes, I'm sure," she said impatiently. "How many times do I have to tell you." And she sat up straight again, a little away from him.

He smiled at her. "I believe you. And I'll express myself properly a little later when we get off this highway."

"It's late," he said. "And cold! This is one of the bad nights."

She leaned forward to peer out the windshield. "I can see the shadow of the castle a distance ahead. It stands out like a grim old spectre against the night."

"You sound as if you don't like it."

"I don't."

"I grew up in it. In many ways it means a great deal to me."

"I can understand that," she said.

As she finished speaking the car engine suddenly gave a kind of odd cough, sputtered and then went dead. Claude looked startled. He said, "What does this mean"

"Could the gas line be frozen?" she asked.

"It never has frozen before," he said. And he tried to get the engine going again but it wouldn't respond. He tried several times and then scanned the dash closely and groaned aloud.

"What is it?" she asked him.

"There's no gas. I've let it run empty of petrol and I was sure I'd put enough in it."

"Well, at least we know what's wrong."

"And we're stuck out here a half mile from the castle," he said with annoyance.

"We can walk back."

"Too cold," he said. "You stay here and keep inside the car. There's still enough warmth to keep you comfortable. I'll hurry back to the garage at the castle. There are spare tins of petrol there."

"I don't mind walking with you," she said.

"No need. Better for you to watch the car," he told her. "I won't be more than fifteen or twenty minutes at the most."

"Whatever you like," she said, resigned.

He smiled. "And I'll take the time to kiss you before I leave. It was very nice hearing that you love me. Just about the best thing I ever heard!" And he drew her close and gave her a kiss which warmed her against the growing chill in the station wagon.

A moment later he was on his way for the gas. She watched him with a wave of emotion filling her and tightening her throat. How good he was! And how lucky she was to have found him! At least something had come of her bizarre adventures in Austria.

She pulled her coat tightly around her and realized that the night was terribly cold. In the few short minutes since Claude had left the temperature had lowered noticeably in the car. She began to feel a kind of claustrophobia. If she could only move around a little, she thought, it would help her circulation and keep her warmer.

At last she came to a decision. She would step outside the car and pace up and down a little. In this way she'd soon feel better. She opened the car door and stepped down onto the snowy road. She tried to catch some sign of Claude in the distance but he had gone too far for her to be able to make out his figure in the darkness.

He had turned out the headlamps to conserve the battery. She walked around by the front of the car and then moved on toward the rear. She pounded her hands together and kept moving to try and fight the biting cold. A slight wind had come up and as it hit her she felt it sting her face so that her eyes pained and began to water a little.

She debated getting back into the front seat of the station wagon once more and then rejected the idea. Claude had promised her that he would be back within fifteen or twenty minutes at the most and already at least five or seven minutes must have gone by. She would soon be encouraged by the sight of him returning along the dark road.

Meanwhile she wished that some other vehicle might come along. Perhaps she could manage to get a lift to the castle if a car showed up. But this road was not much used and at this late hour it was completely deserted. Nothing to do but suffer it out!

She bent her head against the wind as it came again and stood by the front of the car for a moment. Then she thought she heard a sound from behind her and she turned quickly to see a figure on skis about twenty-five feet away from her. She was about to let out a shout of friendly relief and tell the stranger her plight when she took a closer look at him and gasped!

This was no ordinary skier. It was an officer in SS uniform astride the skis. His face was hidden by a stocking mask and strangely distorted as he gazed at her. She could feel the hatred and scorn of his gaze. And then he used his poles as he slid closer toward her.

She gave a cry of fear and started to open the car door, hoping to get inside to some sort of safety. Her hand grasped the door handle and it came open. But not in time! The phantom skier had already grasped her and was hurling her back. She fell down on the icy road with a howl of fear. Now the phantom skier struck at her with one of the poles, viciously jabbing at her. She rolled over quickly to escape the attack.

Once she had a brief glimpse of the face but could not begin to identify who it was behind the mask. He struck at her again and caught her on the shoulder, sending a searing pain through her. She screamed frantically.

And this time her cry was answered by Claude only a short distance away. The sound of his voice calling back to her had a magic effect on her attacker. The skier turned and quickly advanced down the road to a spot where the slope was steep. Then he left the road and a moment later vanished down over the hill.

Clutching her injured shoulder Ina struggled to her feet as Claude came running up to her. Breathlessly he asked, "What was it?"

"The skier," she sobbed. "The phantom skier!"

"What happened to him?"

She pointed. "Down the slope. He's escaped by this time."

Claude asked, "Are you badly hurt?"

"I don't think so. Just my shoulder. He struck me with the pole."

Anger showed on the young man's handsome face. "Did you get a good look at him?"

"He was masked. I couldn't tell what he looked like!"

"I was wrong to leave you," Claude admitted. "Get in the car. I'll put the gas in and with luck we should be on our way in a minute or two."

She did as he suggested and waited in the car as he dumped the gas in from the large can which he'd brought back with him.

Then he quickly got in the car at her side and worked the starter until he got the motor running. After that it was only a few minutes until they reached the castle. He drove around to the rear parking area and they went into the castle by a rear door. He insisted on seeing her injured shoulder and checked the bruise.

"It's bad enough," he said grimly. "And this proves beyond a doubt we have a dangerous lunatic loose in the area. A lunatic on skis."

"He came out of nowhere," she said.

"You didn't recognize his outfit or his build?"

"He was wearing an SS uniform."

Claude sighed. "I'll see the police the first thing in the morning. There can be no doubt that you were attacked by the same person who killed Hans and perhaps somehow murdered my mother and disposed of her body. They'll have to do something about this."

She said, "If they'd only put a night patrol out here he should appear sooner or later."

"I'll expect them to do more than that," he said darkly. "And I think I know who the phantom is."

"Who?"

"You gave me the hint tonight. Rolf Monner! He's an expert skier and he's likely Bruck's son!"

"You've let that idea run away with you."

"We have to start somewhere. We can't let more incidents like the one tonight happen."

"I was terrified beyond belief," she said. "He was working himself up into a frenzy. I'm sure if you hadn't come along he'd have eventually murdered me!"

"It's a bad business," Claude said, his face clouded.

"I'm dead tired," she said. "I must go up to bed."

"I'll see you to your door," Claude told her. "I doubt if the house is even safe now."

As they started up the stairs, she said, "I've told you about that terribly mutilated face I've seen staring at me from the shadows of the house at various times. Do you think he could be the phantom skier?"

"If there is such a character, he might be. At this moment it's anybody's guess," the young man said.

She saw that there wasn't much point in discussing it any further until the morning. She was afraid Claude was too certain the villain was Rolf. She didn't believe this to be true. While she wasn't exactly charmed by the lanky ski instructor, she wasn't sure of his guilt. He just didn't seem the type.

Claude kissed her a tender good night at the door of her room and she went inside feeling a little less tense, though her shoulder was still giving her trouble. She prepared for bed still haunted by the frightening experience in the snow. And after she was in bed she left the lights on. As a precaution she decided to leave them on all night.

The morning was bright and sunny. She felt a little ashamed as she turned off the bedlamp which had burned all night. But at least she'd been able to sleep. She rose and washed and dressed before the maid arrived with her breakfast.

She asked the girl, "Did Miss Gretchen come home last night?"

"Yes, Miss," the maid said. "About ten o'clock. I saw her car come in."

"I wondered," Ina said. She hadn't seen the blonde girl since she'd abandoned her at the hotel dance.

"Everyone is up early this morning," the maid confided. "Mr. Claude has already left for the village and his father is down in the study."

"I think Mr. Claude had an important errand to do," she said.

"Yes," the maid said. "And I've already taken Miss Gretchen her breakfast and she's rarely up at this time."

Ina smiled as she sat down to her breakfast. "What do you think accounts for it?"

"It's hard to say," the maid admitted. "Perhaps what happened to Hans has stirred everyone. I should think they'd be looking for the body of Miss Marta."

"Do the servants believe she is dead?"

"Yes. We all feel she must be."

"It's possible," Ina admitted.

The maid gave her a frightened look. "Cook says she went to the window around midnight last night. She was wakened by screams and she saw the Satan of the Slopes going skiing down the hill from here."

"Is she certain?"

"Yes."

Ina asked, "Have you ever seen the phantom?"

"No, Miss," the girl said nervously. "And I never want to. Those that do see him are as good as dead!"

The maid left after having made this declaration. Ina lingered over her breakfast trying to remember exactly what had been said at the home of the Fesses and what it might mean.

She was thinking of what Pauline Fess had said about seeing Marta's ghost each night when a knock came on her door. She got up and went over and opened it to see Gretchen in a dressing gown standing there.

The blonde girl smiled at her. "Am I allowed to come in?"

"All right," she said.

Gretchen strolled in. "I guess I owe you an apology."

Ina closed the door. "Do you think so?"

Gretchen gave her a look. "I guess you think so, don't you?"

She came over to stand by the girl. "I don't know what to think. You talked me into going to the hotel dance and then you ran off with that Englishman and left me."

The blonde girl went over to a chair and sank down into it with a sigh. She gave Ina a resigned look. "Rotten of me, wasn't it? I'll admit it. But you see there was this party at a friend of Jim's in the village."

"You could have told me."

Gretchen waved a hand placatingly. "Don't get ahead of me. I would have but we didn't plan to be gone long. We only intended to stay at the party for a little while."

"But you didn't?"

The pretty blonde grimaced. "You know how these things are. The time went by quicker than we expected. Before I knew it I saw it was seven. I decided it was no use going to the hotel; that you'd have left by then anyway."

She said grimly, "How did you think I'd get back here? Walk?"

Gretchen smiled. "You're too attractive to have to resort to anything like that. I knew you'd get a lift from somebody."

"I wish I'd had your confidence. It would have saved me a lot of worry."

"You didn't have to worry. Rolf drove you home."

Ina showed surprise. "How do you know that?"

"He told me," Gretchen said, a roguish light in her blue eyes.

"Where did you see him?"

"At the party. He came to it after he left you. We were all there until about ten; then I drove back here."

Ina said, "If it hadn't been for Rolf, I don't know what I would have done."

Gretchen smiled at her. "You've really got him at your feet. He's crazy about you."

"Really?"

"Yes. He talked about you all night. He even broke his long silence with me. He thinks I may be able to help him with you since he knows we're cousins."

Ina gave her a cynical look. "You can tell him from me that you have no influence with me at all. Especially after last night."

Gretchen rose from the chair. "Don't make a big thing out of it."

"It was a big thing for me," she said.

"I hear you and Claude went out together for the evening," the blonde said. "I'd say you have no shortage of admirers. You ought to be able to have your pick. Why don't you forget the book and marry Rolf or Claude?"

"You may not believe it," she said. "But I don't happen to be interested in marriage at the moment."

"The book is the big thing? Is that it?"

"The book and my career in general," Ina said.

"I think you're making a mistake," her blonde cousin told her. "But it's your life. I'll see you later. I just wanted to be sure there were no hard feelings." And she went out before Ina could make any further comment.

CHAPTER ELEVEN

Ina finished her breakfast coffee and then went downstairs to do some work on the papers in Marta's room. She reached the door just in time to have it open in her face and see a strained-looking Kate Bromley emerge. The big woman gave her a curt nod and hurried on.

She called after her, "I won't have to unlock the door since you've left it open." Then she went on in to Marta's ornate bedroom. She'd only advanced a few steps when she halted and let out a small cry of disbelief. The room was a mess! It had been ransacked and torn up as if a madman had gone through it seeking something. All the drawers were out of the desk and the carpet was a mess of papers!

There was nothing in the bedroom which had escaped being torn up. She stared around her in consternation. All the sorting out she'd done had been lost. Papers were strewn everywhere. She didn't know where she'd begin again. And then as the first stunning shock left her she recalled her meeting with Kate Bromley in the doorway of the room. And the big woman had been behaving strangely. Had she done this mischief?

A wave of anger rose in her and she turned and left the room quickly. She made her way downstairs and directly to the study where she hoped to find David Leopold. When she reached the door to the study she saw the old man seated at his desk while Kate Bromley stood before him evidently recounting her version of what had happened.

As Ina strode into the room the big Englishwoman turned to glance at her with a frightened look and at once stopped talking. Ina continued on in until she was also standing directly in front of David Leopold.

The old man gave her a troubled look. "I suppose you have come to repeat the bad news Miss Bromley has just given me."

She said, "The room has been ransacked. Everything is in a mess."

"So Miss Bromley says," he told her.

Ina turned to Kate Bromley with an angry glance. "What were you doing in there?"

The big woman bridled. "I have a right to go in there when I please. I am Marta Landen's secretary."

"I thought the room was to be my responsibility while I was working there," Ina told Leopold. "How do I know this woman didn't deliberately turn the room upside down to make my task more difficult?"

"Don't you dare accuse me of a thing like that!" Kate Bromley said, her broad face crimson.

"I've said what I was thinking," Ina declared.

David Leopold rose, his lined face showing strain. "Now, ladies, we mustn't have this kind of quarreling between you. I'm quite certain neither of you is to blame for what has happened."

"Then why did she accuse me?" Kate asked angrily.

"Why were you in the room?" Ina wanted to know.

"It is my right."

"Not while I'm supposed to have the sole key," she said.

David Leopold came over between them. "We must not argue among ourselves," he said. "Let us face what has happened intelligently. Someone deliberately messed up the room to make it harder for Miss Sperling to assemble the materials for her book."

"That has to be true," Ina agreed.

"I had nothing to do with it," Kate Bromley said. "I

went in there to get a typewriter ribbon from the desk. And I found the room turned upside down."

"Well," David Leopold said, "it seems whoever is at the bottom of this has done his worst."

"It may be worse than we guess," Ina was quick to point out. "It may be that whoever did this awful thing has also made off with some of the papers."

"I hope not," David Leopold said, but he looked worried. "The question now is how to begin to restore order in the room. I can have a maid go up and clean as well as she can."

"Not before I gather up the papers scattered around," Ina said. "I have an idea the maid might not value them as we do."

"Very well," the old man said. "You and Miss Bromley join your efforts in gathering up the papers. Then when you are finished I will have a maid clean the room and set it in order. Does that sound logical?"

"Yes," she said. "If Miss Bromley is willing to work with me?"

Kate Bromley said, "I will if you'll apologize for accusing me of upsetting the room."

Ina considerd this and decided it would be better to have Kate Bromley on her side if she could. So she said, "I'm sorry. I was shocked and all I could think of was seeing you leave the room."

David Leopold gave a rare smile. "There, you see. Your differences are all arranged as I'm sure they will be in the future."

"Shall we start with the papers at once?" Ina asked.

"Please do," he implored her. "And no more of this arguing between you."

They left the room in silence. As Ina mounted the stairs the big woman puffed along at her side. And at the last they were on their knees on the floor working together. Getting up all the sheets of paper proved a monumental task.

"Where shall I put these?" the big woman asked as she paused with her hands full of white and yellow sheets.

"Fill the desk drawers and put any surplus on the top of the desk," Ina told her. "Later I'll start the job of sorting the material. Just now we want to gather up what we can."

"Yes, Miss," Kate Bromley said. "It was a dreadful thing to do to Miss Landen's room and a blow to you."

"I'm getting used to such happenings," she said as she worked.

They worked the entire morning in the room. Once they were visited by Leopold. He moved about the room sputtering his anger at whoever did the damage. And he told them, "I intend to find the person responsible for this."

After he'd gone Ina said grimly, "I wouldn't like to place any large bets on his doing so."

"And I agree," Kate Bromley said. "Mister David is too easy and so we have something like this happen."

They worked on for a while longer and their next visitor was Gretchen. The blonde girl had donned a smart brown pants suit and was at her most annoying as she swaggered around the room.

"Well!" she exclaimed. "Someone really did it!"

Ina paused on her knees to ask, "Want to help?"

"You must be joking," the blonde said. "What a silly idea!"

"Then please just don't remain here giving out brilliant remarks," Ina told her. "We're busy."

"That's right, Miss Gretchen," Kate Bromley joined in. The big woman had worked so hard, Ina was sorry she'd ever tried to accuse her of the mischief. It showed how easy it was to make a serious mistake.

"Mother must have come back and done this just to show you," Gretchen jeered.

"You think so?" Ina asked.

"Who else? This looks like her work. Alive or dead she knows how to even a score. You'd better remember that."

Ina said, "Why should she want to even a score with me?"

"You interfered with the material she had ready for her book without her permission," Gretchen commented.

"You seem to know a great deal about it," Ina said with meaning.

"Mere guessing," Gretchen taunted. Then she left the room.

Kate Bromley stared after the departed Gretchen grimly and said, "I wouldn't be at all surprised if she had something to do with this."

"Perhaps," Ina agreed as she gathered more papers and tried to straighten them out to sort later. "She might have done it out of spite."

"There's plenty of that in her," Kate said gloomily. "What Marta Landen put up with from that young hussy few people know."

Ina didn't encourage any dreary revelations from the stout woman. She felt it wiser to allow Kate to direct all her energies into gathering the papers. At last they finished that part of the clearing up of the room. Now the maids could take over.

Ina placed heavy books on the papers on top of the desk and then turned to thank a weary Kate Bromley. She said, "Without your help I wouldn't be done by now."

"What will you do if it happens again?" the big woman asked.

Ina looked at the desk grimly. "I'll take the first plane back to New York," she said and she meant it.

When she washed and changed into another outfit she went downstairs and had luncheon with David Leopold, Gretchen and Claude. She could tell that Claude was tense but he said nothing to her at the table. They didn't even speak of the mess in the bedroom; instead the table conversation was confined to small talk about the weather and the influx of visitors for the Alpine Mardi Gras.

"I hear there are more here than ever for this year's festival," David Leopold said with a sigh. "It will be the first time we haven't had the costume ball here. But without Marta it would be a mockery."

Gretchen looked up from her plate. "Otto Fess and his wife are taking over the costume ball. They wrote and invited me."

"I have also received an invitation," her father said. "But unless Marta returns safely I will not attend. They sent us the invitations only out of politeness. They could not expect us to attend with things as they are."

Gretchen glared at him defiantly. "I intend to go no matter what," she said.

David Leopold sighed but said nothing.

As soon as luncheon was over Claude took Ina into the music room and told her, "I've seen the police and told them about last night."

"And?"

"And they've promised to take some action."

"Such as?" she asked.

"They are going to investigate Rolf Monner and they'll have a man on duty in the vicinity of the castle every night. How is your injured shoulder?"

She grimaced. "I didn't have time to think about it. Somebody turned Marta's room upside down and it took Kate Bromley and I all morning to simply gather the papers from the floor and furniture. When I'll get them in order again I can't predict."

Claude looked shocked. "That's a nice development!"

"And as if that weren't bad enough, Gretchen came in to taunt me as I worked. She suggested her mother had returned, either alive or dead, and deliberately caused the mess."

Claude said, "More likely it was her."

"I've been thinking the same thing."

"I'm sorry," he said.

She turned to stare out the window of the music room at the snow-covered hillside. "I often wonder why I ever made this trip to Austria."

"I think it was fated."

She turned again with a brief smile for him. "Do you?" Her hand reached up to the lapel of his jacket.

"Yes. Otherwise we wouldn't have met."

"That's true."

"And when we get to the bottom of whatever is going on

here things will be different. We'll have some time for ourselves."

"I hope so," she said. "You keep saying that but the mysteries are never solved and new ones come along."

"It has to change," the young violinist said. He placed a hand on hers and touched his lips to her forehead. "Do you think you'd enjoy the life of a traveling musician? That's the life you'd have to share with me. I will have to go on giving tours."

"I've always liked to travel," she told him.

"Then we'll have no quarrels," he said.

"Our problem is not in the future," she said. "But now. How we manage here. Whether we find out what happened to your mother. And whether I ever finish the book about her. I'm beginning to see a kind of pattern of things."

He frowned. "In what way?"

She said, "I think whoever caused her to vanish and attacked Hans and killed him and tried to attack me did so for a definite reason. The same reason that Marta's room was ransacked."

"Go on," he said.

"It has to do with the book. Somebody is afraid of what Marta intended to write about them. They are out to stop the book at any cost so a few lives more or less mean nothing to them."

"You're probably right," Claude agreed.

"There can be no other explanation. And it may be why some people thought Marta was afraid just before she vanished. She may have known the risk she was taking but not minded since she was determined to bring back her stardom through the publicity of the book."

He nodded. "So the more sensational things she wrote about people, the better she hoped it would sell. And the more it sold the greater her chance of being in the limelight once more and getting some important screen roles!"

"That sums it up," Ina said. "Except for one thing."

"What?"

"So far I haven't come across anything that sensational in the material I've read."

Claude looked interested. "Maybe you're still to come to those notes."

"Perhaps. But I think the mysterious marauder had to be searching for that same sensational material. And I doubt if they found it."

"Why?"

She gave him an earnest glance. "I've got a hunch Marta hid the best of the material somewhere as soon as she became frightened. Your father had an idea she'd sent some things to me in New York. But she hadn't. I checked with my mother on long distance."

"Which means?"

"That the sensational material is still here in St. Anton. She's hidden it somewhere and not likely in her room. Perhaps somewhere in the house."

Claude said, "If she's dead no one may ever locate it."

"That could be possible," she said. "So the killer may have accomplished what he sought without ever realizing it. It is unlikely the book I can assemble from what I have now will ever hurt anyone."

Claude said, "So if Rolf Monner is doing all this to protect his father's name, he's wasting his effort."

"I don't think the culprit is Rolf."

"Why?"

"I just don't see him as a violent type. And we don't know that he's Karl Bruck's son. That's just your guess."

"I'm a gambler. I've a hunch I'm right. Want to give me odds?"

She shook her head. "Not at this point."

"So what happens next?"

Ina gave him a look of rueful amusement. "I'm going to have to begin sorting out all those notes again. Want to help me?"

"No!" he said.

But actually he did help some. She worked at the task days and evenings for almost a week. And for a good deal of the time Claude was at her side. He became interested in his mother's memoirs and they broke the monotony of their work by discussing some of the incidents from time to time.

He said, "Here's one about Emil Jannings. She was very fond of him and thought he was the one who really made the 'Blue Angel' the success it was, not Dietrich. And we all know that Jannings was liked pretty well by the Nazis."

"I've been told it ruined his postwar career in America," she said. "At least Marta avoided that pitfall. She's written a long item about my Uncle Ralph but somehow I get the impression she respected his talents as a playwright more than she loved him as a husband."

Claude asked, "What about the anti-Nazi play he was supposed to have been writing? The one that got lost after his death. Does she say anything about that?"

"No. She's mysteriously silent about that play."

"It figures," he said with a grim expression.

"What?"

"My foster mother was a Nazi. She married David and adopted me as a means to keep her picture popularity. Somehow she came to care for both of us. I owe everything to her. But I still have to face that she did it purely from selfish motives."

Ina smiled at him sympathetically. "Don't you know a lot of good deeds manage to get done the same way? Are the motives so important if the results turn out well?"

"Maybe not."

"What will you say to her if she returns?"

The young man shook his head grimly. "She won't return. Not after this long while. She has to be dead."

"She likely is. Maybe it's best that way. I don't think this book she planned would have done all she expected for her career. Even if it had sensational material, the public that would read it is not the public she knew. There's a different audience today and I don't think her memoirs would have any interest for them."

"I worried about that from the start," he admitted.

"So what shall I do? I may write the book out of curiosity to see how it is received."

"You can research many of the facts on your own. For instance, there must be many files available on Karl Bruck and the Nazi crowd in general. You could cull material from that type of source."

"I know," she agreed. "I'll be able to decide better if we are able to capture the maniac posing as the phantom skier."

"The police have promised to work hard on that aspect of things," he said.

"I hope they mean it this time."

"I think they do."

It appeared that the police did mean it. For that night she and Claude drove to the village for awhile in the station wagon. And both ways they saw the policeman on duty in his jeep. It was comforting to know that the castle and the grounds were being watched. Ina relaxed and made good progress in getting the notes Marta had left in order.

Some of the frightening atmosphere seemed to have vanished from the old castle with the knowledge there was always a policeman on duty. And it seemingly had its effect on the phantom as well. There were no more appearances by him nor were there any new attacks.

When Ina thought she had the notes in fair shape, she had a meeting in the study with David Leopold. "I have everything fairly well organized," she said. "But there are strange lapses in the sequence which makes me believe Marta deliberately skipped some parts of her life or wrote them and had them stolen from her. Did she ever mention such a loss to you?"

"No," Marta's husband said. "She never complained about it and I'm sure she would have if anything had been stolen. She was very touchy on that subject."

"There is another possibility," she said.

"Yes?"

"She may have written some special material which she's

hidden somewhere because she was threatened with its being stolen or just frightened about the possibility."

Leopold looked upset. "From what you hint this could be very sensational material?"

"It could."

"And Marta likely hid it before she vanished?"

"Yes."

"Any idea where?" he asked.

"No."

"Then if Marta doesn't return, it may be forever lost?"

Ina nodded. "I suppose so."

The old man sighed. "Perhaps it is better that way."

"I'm not certain of that either."

"Why do you say that?"

She looked at his lined face with solemn eyes. "Because it also means that some of the most important sections of the book are missing. Especially the parts dealing with the Nazis."

David Leopold seemed worried. "I prefer not to have any mention of my wife's friendship with those people. She lived to regret those days and wanted to forget them."

Ina shook her head. "Sorry. You have it all wrong."

The old man's mouth gaped open. "Please explain that."

"I think those were the days that counted for her. She lived them over in her memory. But she could always face grim facts when they were grim enough. So she decided to tell all about the Nazi escapades so long as it gave her new theatrical life."

David Leopold gasped. "How can you interpret what my dear Marta thought? You are substituting your own thoughts!"

"No," she said, "I'm merely giving Marta's thoughts life."

"Whatever, I want to think she hated her Nazi days."

"I think you're wrong."

David Leopold was agitated. "If you do the book I want no mention of Nazis or that awful man!"

"You mean Karl Bruck?"

"Yes. No mention of him at all!"

"Then the book would be fraudulent and wouldn't interest me," she explained.

"Why not?"

"I have to tell her whole story, not part of it. People know she came back to Germany during the war and that she was the darling of Hitler and his crew. If we left all that out of the book every critic would jeer at the omission and you'd do Marta much more harm than good."

"A chance I'd be willing to take," the old man said.

"I can't see the sense in it," she said. "Marta is likely dead. What harm could such revelations cause? Bruck is also dead, as are most of the Nazis of that time."

"I still don't like it being flouted that Marta knew all those scoundrels!"

"I'm sorry," she said. "If I agree to do the book it has to be on my terms."

"I will make the decisions," the old man said angrily. "And I intend to protect Marta."

"You'll simply be wrecking her career," she objected.

"If she returns I'm positive she'll understand."

"I wouldn't count on that," she said.

"You seem to think you know a lot about my wife. More than perhaps I do."

"It's possible," she said coolly.

He stared at her uncertainly for a moment. Then his upset and anger seemed to drain from him and he sank down in his chair merely a weary old man.

He said, "But then you are the expert on books."

"I like to think so," she said.

"I have you here all the way from America," he went on. "So I may as well take your advice."

"I wish you would. Otherwise I'll pass the book by."

"Marta wanted you to do it."

"I believe that. It's the only reason I've held on this long," she said.

"Please continue," he begged her.

"My plan is to get all the information on Karl Bruck and the Nazis closest to him from reliable files. I will then piece the story together as best I can. Pauline Fess was a friend of Marta's in those days. No doubt she'll be able to help."

He scowled. "Don't count on it. Pauline's mind is blurred. She is suffering from hardened arteries."

"Often such people have oddly lucid spells. And at those times they recall vividly."

"You think Pauline might be valuable to you?"

"Yes. If her husband doesn't interfere."

David Leopold nodded. "I know. He is a strange fellow. One of the Hitler gang himself. He will not let her talk too freely. Be sure of that."

"I can at least try to get an appointment with her," she said. "He is anxious for us all to attend his Mardi Gras party. So he should court our good will."

"His holding the party is an insult to Marta, who may be ill or dead somewhere."

"Still he intends to have it. Have I your permission to contact him?"

The old man waved a hand wearily. "Do you require it?"

"Yes," Ina said. "I want your blessing on this all the way."

"All right," he said. "Talk to Pauline. But watch Otto. He could be nasty."

"I've found that out already," she said.

"What if you get all the facts you wish?"

"I'll put them in written form and have you check them."

Pain showed in David Leopold's face. "What if it becomes evident that Marta hated Jews and joined in the persecution of them? How will that make her marriage to me look?"

Ina said, "It will only prove she gradually achieved some sort of mental maturity. It can't possibly reflect on you."

"You say that. But are you just mouthing words?" the old man asked.

"I believe firmly in what I'm saying," she told him. "As proof of where I stand, Claude and I plan to be married when all this is settled."

The old man looked startled. "You mean it?"

"Yes."

"I had no idea!"

"Do you approve?"

"But of course," David Leopold said. "Claude is a most fortunate young man and you are a remarkable girl. I wonder how I could have been blind to this budding romance."

"You have had other worries," she said.

Her revelation seemed to leave the old man more resigned. He said, "Very well. I shouldn't have begun to lay down rules. Do the book as you think best."

"Be sure that I'll try to be fair," she promised him.

"I have never questioned that," David Leopold said.

Instead of phoning Otto Fess she decided to go over and visit him. She got the car keys from Claude and drove over to the smaller castle in the station wagon. In the daytime the Fess place looked even more strikingly like the castle.

A male servant answered the door and let her in. She waited in the reception hall while the servant went to get Otto Fess. She studied the walls of the hall which were hung with dark tapestries and especially noted a suit of ancient armor on a stand in one corner of it.

After a moment she heard a dry cough and footsteps on the stairs. Then the gaunt Otto Fess came into view. He descended the stairs looking more the arrogant Prussian than anyone she'd ever seen.

He came across the room to her with those cold eyes holding an inquiring look. He said, "Yes, Miss Sperling?"

"Please forgive me for coming here without a phone call or anything to let you know," she apologized.

He stood there stiffly, his gray tweed suit about the same shade as his close-cropped hair. He said, "It doesn't matter to me. I regret, however, that my wife is not well today and will not be able to see you."

"I am disappointed," she said.

"Well, Pauline has her good days and bad ones," the grim old man told her.

She said, "It is about Pauline I'd like to talk to you."

He frowned slightly. "Let us go into my study; it will be more comfortable."

Ina followed him into the ground-floor study. It was a huge room lined with books with a stone fireplace at one end. And over the fireplace was a large framed oil painting of Adolph Hitler. She'd barely taken this in when she noticed that on the old man's library table there was a framed and autographed photo of Rudolph Hess.

She at once went to it and studied the gaunt features of the Nazi leader. Then she turned to Otto Fess and said, "I had no idea you knew Rudolph Hess intimately."

The old man was studying her grimly. He said, "We met at a function in Berlin once. He was amused that my name was so close to his. Out of this chance meeting a friendship was born and we saw each other many times later. It was not a political friendship. He was kind enough to send me that photo."

"How very interesting," she said.

"I'm rather proud of it."

"And Hess is the only one left, I mean of all the group ruling at that time. Do you suppose they'll ever set him free?"

"It is a cruel injustice to keep him in prison," Otto Fess said stiffly.

"Your painting of Hitler is excellent as well. Isn't it by the same artist who did Marta and Karl Bruck?"

The old man turned to study the painting. "Yes. I bought all three at the same time. Even though one may have questioned Hitler as a leader, he was a most interesting person."

"I agree," she said. "Even today that is true. I'd like to carry some of the flavor of those times in the book I plan to do about Marta."

"You are going ahead with the book then?" he said.

"Yes. David Leopold thinks I should."

"Indeed," the old man's tone hinted of sarcasm.

She stared at him. "You sound disapproving?"

He shrugged. "I hardly like to venture an opinion. But I feel you should be sure of what happened to Marta before you begin the book."

"I think she's dead."

"But you do not know that as a fact."

"Even her husband is coming around to that point of view."

"So you plan to begin the book?"

"Yes. I have a great deal of material from Marta's notes. But there are omissions. Grave omissions!"

Otto Fess scowled. "What sort of omissions?"

"There is nothing about her days in Nazi Germany nor any mention of Karl Bruck. It is as if that period in her life didn't exist."

The gaunt man said, "Then she probably didn't want that in the book."

"I disagree. I think she wrote the section and in a sensational way. It was her main bid for reader attention. I have an idea she made revelations that haven't been printed before."

"Then why haven't you found the notes on them?"

"Because they were either stolen or she hid them because she was threatened if she planned to use them. I'm not sure which. I only know that they are missing."

"So?"

"To balance the book I hope to recreate that period. I may not be able to offer all the revelations Marta might have made but I will be able to include that vital period of her life. I will consult newspaper and magazine files and more importantly rely on people like your wife and you who were friends of hers at that time to help fill in many of the missing details."

The old man stared at her angrily. "You're asking me to tell you about those days?"

"Yes."

"I do not admit they existed," he declared. "It is a time I wish to forget."

She nodded toward the painting of Hitler and then

glanced at the autographed photo of Rudolph Hess. "Judging by the evidence in here, you have not forgotten."

Otto Fess took a step toward her, his gaunt face livid. "Is that an amateurish attempt at blackmail, Miss Sperling?"

"No. I'm merely pointing out a fact. Why should you be ashamed that you were a Nazi? Everyone makes mistakes. Marta did and she remedied hers by marrying David Leopold and adopting Claude. You can balance the past by helping me with my book. I'm sure your wife would be willing to help."

"Then you are wrong," he said in a cutting tone. "We want no part of your project. I do not wish to quarrel with you but I will not have any such intrusion of my privacy. Is that understood?"

"You make it very plain," she said.

"Then there is no more to say."

She hesitated, then told him, "Perhaps one thing. If in my other research I come upon any information about you I will use it. You'd better be prepared for that."

"I have an excellent lawyer, Miss Sperling," the old man said. "I advise you to tread carefully in this matter."

"I understand," she said. "Thank you and good afternoon."

He saw her to the reception hall and helped her on with her coat. In a somewhat milder tone he said, "I trust you understand that I meant nothing personal in this. I wish no quarrel with you."

She gave him a serious look. "I feel exactly the same way."

"I do have to protect my privacy and I intend to."

"Of course."

"As for poor Pauline, she is not responsible mentally. So I must act as a sort of guardian in her case."

"At least you've made your position clear," she said. "David Leopold had hoped you would help."

"David Leopold and I are acquaintances rather than close friends," the old man said icily. "He could never know my viewpoint. My friendship was with Marta."

She left him standing in the doorway watching her as she got into the station wagon. She had a weird feeling that his eyes were malevolently fixed on her. He was still standing there as she drove off along the snowy road.

So this was the Austria she was faced with. Not a land of gaiety, music and *palatschinen,* but a cold, grimly remembering place. Her corner of Austria was filled with exiles from Nazi Germany—bitter individuals who had gathered here to live in seclusion and remember their days of greatness. Marta had been their image of glamour long lost—and now Marta herself was missing.

A troubling thought struck her as she drove the station wagon past the village with its quaint eighteenth-century architecture. Claude had pointed out that Rolf Monner's eyes matched those of the dead Karl Bruck almost exactly. But just now she had seen other eyes identical to those of the dead Nazi leader. The icy eyes of Otto Fess!

CHAPTER TWELVE

Claude was waiting for her at the castle. As soon as she took off her coat they went into the music room which seemed their favorite place to talk. He closed the doors so they would have privacy and then faced her.

"Well?"

She grimaced. "A wasted call."

"Oh"

"Yes. Otto Fess refuses to cooperate. He will not talk about the Hitler era or his friendship with Marta in those days. Nor will he allow Pauline to help me."

The musician's handsome face clouded. "I'm not surprised."

"In his study there is a painting of Hitler and an autographed copy of a photo of Rudolf Hess. He's living in the memory of those days like all the others! He and Marta and who knows how many more in this village are living in a phantom world of yesterday's Germany. No wonder the locals talk of the Phantom of the Slopes! It fits!"

"You're discouraged?"

"Not really. I'll go ahead without the help of Otto Fess or Pauline. I've always been considered a first-class researcher. This will give me a chance to prove it."

Claude gave her a smile of encouragement. "I like your spirit."

She smiled back at him. "Do you like me? That's more important."

"Delighted to prove it," he said, and he put his arms around her and gave her a tender kiss.

She stared at him dreamily. "I can't believe any of this. It's all happening so differently from what I expected."

"That's often true in life."

"I wish I knew what Marta did with those missing notes," she said.

Claude sighed. "So does the phantom, whoever he is."

"She must have told something in them. Something this phantom could not afford to have made public."

The young man eyed her mockingly. "Say it is the ghost of Karl Bruck returned to avenge Marta for wanting to betray him."

She gave him an interested look. "In a way that is just it."

"Go on," he said.

"The other day you said that Rolf had Karl Bruck's eyes. I can tell you someone else who has them."

"Who?"

"Otto Fess."

"You just think that because he's a Nazi and cold."

"No," she said, "I mean it. The eyes are identical. I say this because I don't want you blaming Rolf for everything. I think he's innocent."

"And I say he's Karl Bruck's son, legitimate or illegitimate."

She sighed. "You don't give up an idea easily."

"No."

She glanced over at his violin. "You haven't been playing much lately?"

"Too many pressures."

"You should get back to it," she warned him. "You need to keep at it a certain number of hours a day."

"I do some playing in the early morning before you are up," he said. "Mostly exercises."

She glanced at the organ. "No one plays the organ now."

"It is kept locked," he said. "Mother was the one who played it when she was here. She was very good."

She eyed him thoughtfully. "Yet I was sure I heard it

being played that first night I was here. Could it have been ghostly hands?"

"Overwrought nerves," he said.

"I wonder."

"You've hated this house from the start," Claude said.

"I think I have," she agreed. "I came here expecting to find Marta and she had vanished." Her eyes met his. "Do you think she'll return?"

"I don't know," he sighed.

"It's going to be very hard on your father if she doesn't," Ina said.

"I realize that."

"I think even Gretchen will feel her loss."

Claude looked grim. "Your beloved cousin has gone off with her English boy friend again. He called for her while you were out."

"It begins to seem serious."

"I wouldn't count on it," Claude said. "I've talked with him. A slippery type."

Ina gave him a sharp glance. "Have you ever thought of this? That Gretchen and her boy friend might be behind the abducting and killings? She has a motive. She hated her mother."

Claude looked surprised. "Next you'll be including me as a suspect, or Father!"

"No, I mean it about Gretchen," she insisted. "Think about it."

The balance of the day went by without event. Ina noted that Gretchen did not return for the evening meal. David Leopold seemed troubled and behaved as if his mind were a distance away. Ina worked on her notes into the early evening as Claude had some letters to write in connection with the temporary cancellation of his tour.

Kate Bromley came into Marta's bedroom to offer any assistance she could and it was then that Ina queried her about the early Nazi days when she had lived in Germany. She asked Kate, "Did you know Marta in those days?"

The big woman shook her head. "Not until the war ended. I was unemployed and ready to give up and return to England. Miss Landen rescued me. She gave me work and a home with her."

Ina said, "Then you must have known Karl Bruck?"

"I read of him in the papers," the woman said. "He was dead by the time I came here. He died with Hitler in Berlin."

"I know," Ina agreed. "But I thought you might have joined Marta before that."

"Not until later."

"Did she ever talk to you about Karl Bruck?"

Kate Bromley hesitated. "I suppose his name was mentioned. But she never went into any details about their friendship."

"So you can't help fill in any facts for me?"

"I'm sure Miss Landen wrote about all that."

"Perhaps, but the notes are missing."

Kate Bromley's broad face showed annoyance. "Perhaps whoever tore up this room stole them?"

"Possibly."

"Is there anything else?" the big woman asked.

"Not at the moment," Ina said, dismissing her.

She had strangely mixed views about Kate Bromley. While the aging Englishwoman had been an avowed Nazi, at least she was honest about it. And Ina felt she was probably also honest in most other things. The lonely spinster had been devoted to Marta and surely missed her as much as anyone else in the castle. But Ina also realized she couldn't count on the woman for an unprejudiced picture of that period in Germany before the Second World War.

At ten o'clock Claude came up and sat with her awhile. Then he saw her to her room. She prepared for bed quite exhausted and turned off the lights and went directly into a sound sleep.

She wakened with the room still dark but with that eerie sense that she was being spied on again. She listened for some betraying sound but there was only the wind.

After a while she decided to get up and go as far as the hallway. She was too uneasy to go back to sleep.

Putting on her dressing gown and slippers, she went out into the hall. And again she had the feeling that she was not alone. She went as far as the head of the stairs and it was there she heard the organ in the music room being played faintly behind closed doors. But she was sure it was the organ she was hearing.

Her hand on the bannister, she cautiously advanced down the stairway; when she reached the lower hall the sound of the organ behind the closed doors of the music room was much louder. There could be no question that someone was in there playing it. Either Marta, her ghost or someone else who had the keys.

Fear on her pretty face, she moved slowly toward the door. And just as she touched the door handle the music ceased abruptly. It both baffled and frustrated her. She turned the handle and opened the door. The room was dark and seemingly empty! She reached in to the nearest light switch and turned the chandelier on overhead. Now the room was bathed in soft light but still she saw no one. But she was certain unseen eyes were taking in her every movement. It was a dreadful feeling.

She stood in the music room for a few minutes and then turned off the lights and closed the door. Again in the shadowed hall she debated about going upstairs or whether to roam around on the ground floor. It was almost as if she were being guided by some master puppeteer. She moved down the hallway until she reached the entrance to the drawing room.

All the lights in the room were out except the lights over the fine oil paintings which remained on both day and night. Her eyes fixed on the full-length painting of Marta and it seemed that the fabled star was smiling at her mockingly in return. She was standing there transfixed by the ghostly countenance of the missing woman when she heard the floor board creak sharply behind her.

With a start she turned quickly to find herself gazing into horror. A few feet behind her lurked the phantom creature she'd seen so many times before. The thing with the horribly disfigured face, the mouth lost in scar tissue, the eyes burning madly. The thing uttered a croaking sound as its filthy hands stretched out toward her.

It was more than Ina could bear and she screamed out her terror and backed into the drawing room. Now the thing with long, gray matted hair reaching to its shoulders came stalking her. She screamed again and again as she found herself threatened.

She continued to retreat as the phantom came nearer and the grimy hands with the dirty broken fingernails groped for her throat. She was sobbing and screaming at the same time as he grasped her and began throttling her. She stared up into the hideous face with horrified eyes.

Then she heard other sounds and Claude's voice and a moment later the young man had pounced on the phantom thing, struggling with him and dragging him away from her. She collapsed on the floor in weeping misery.

Now David Leopold was beside her and the lights were turned on. The old man was sympathetic as he patted her shoulder. "You poor child!" he said.

"That thing! The horrible thing!" she sobbed.

"I know," he said.

Now Claude had returned to help her to her feet and into a nearby chair. He knelt by her and asked, "Did he harm you in any way?"

"Just terrified me," she sobbed. "Who was it?"

Claude turned to eye his father sternly. He said, "Well, you'd better tell her."

David Leopold stood before her with a guilty expression on his lined face. He said, "I'm sorry. The man who attacked you has been living here all the while. We all knew about him, except you. We decided not to tell you since you might only be upset."

"What do you mean?" she asked.

"The man is a servant who worked for Marta before the war. He was almost burned to death in a bombing and emerged from the ordeal badly disfigured and retarded mentally. But Marta would not give him up so she kept him on to do odd jobs here and saw that he was given accommodation where he could have privacy."

"He's been spying on me ever since I arrived and tonight he attacked me," she told them indignantly.

"He somehow got it into his head that you were responsible for Marta's vanishing," Claude explained. "I straightened him out on it and you won't be bothered any more."

"I should hope not," she said.

"You don't need to worry about it," the old man assured her. "We'll send him away tomorrow. He should have been in a mental hospital long ago."

Claude saw her back upstairs again. He said, "I feel guilty that I was one of the conspirators in this case."

She gave him a troubled look. "How do I know you won't turn out to be at fault again?"

"You'll have to take my word for it."

She said, "Before he attacked me I heard the organ playing in the music room." They were standing by her door.

The young man stared at her. "You're harping on that again?"

"It's true. I heard the music clearly."

"I don't know," he said. "I don't understand it. I guess there must be a ghost in this house."

"Do you know what I think?" she asked.

"No."

"I think the house is full of ghosts. Grim Nazi ghosts!"

Claude smiled wryly. "Maybe they're avoiding me on religious grounds. I'll have to keep a sharper look." On that note they said good night.

The time of the costume ball at the home of Otto Fess was getting nearer and the police had still not come up with any more news about the phantom skier or the missing Marta.

Ina worked on and the book was starting to take shape. Then one evening she received a phone call from the brash

Rolf Monner. He said, "We haven't seen each other for too long. I'm coming by to pick you up tonight."

She was at once on guard. "No, I think not."

"I won't be refused," the young German said. "I'll be by at nine. I don't get off until eight."

"I make no promises," she warned him.

"You'll be waiting for me," he told her in an amused yet assured tone.

She put down the phone with misgivings and immediately returned to Claude with whom she'd been talking before the phone call came in.

She said, "Guess what?"

Claude shrugged. "That's getting to be a tired game here."

"I've had a call from Rolf," she said, and went on to tell him the details.

Claude shocked her by saying, "I think you should keep the date with him."

"Why?" she gasped.

A smile flickered at his lips. "It might be just what we want. It could be that he'll reveal something more about himself to you tonight. He wants to marry you, so he claims. So let him fill in his background for you. The stupid local police haven't had any luck. But then they don't do anything."

"You want me to meet him?" she asked soberly.

"I think it would be smart."

"How about dangerous?"

"No," Claude rationalized. "He has to call here to pick you up. We'll make it clear we all know you're with him. Even if he is the phantom, he daren't harm you tonight."

"I hope you're right," she said.

"I wouldn't allow you to go with him if I thought anything else," Claude said.

She was still hesitant. "I feel we should discuss it with your father."

"You don't trust my judgment?"

"No," she said. "I want a second opinion."

"All right," he said.

They found the old man at his desk in the study. He beckoned them to sit down with him and said, "There is an air of conspiracy about you two. What is it now?"

She smiled wanly. "Claude wants me to go out on a date with Rolf Monner. I'm not too anxious."

David Leopold showed shock. "But Claude and you are about to become engaged, why should he want that? Or have you already changed your minds about each other?"

Claude smiled at her. "It's nothing like that," he told his father.

"Then I wish you would explain," the old man said.

"It's simply that I think Rolf Monner is the phantom skier," Claude said. "I think he killed Mother and has hidden her body somewhere and I think he's responsible for Hans' death and has tried to murder Ina."

"So you are planning to have her go out on a date with him?" the old man said with sarcasm.

"Yes," Claude said. "As long as it is in the open. He'll not dare hurt her if we all know she's with him. And she may be able to find out something about him. I think he's Karl Bruck's son."

David Leopold looked astounded. "Did Karl Bruck have a son?"

"We're not sure," Ina said. "I doubt it. It's just a theory of Claude's."

"And I'd like to have a chance to prove it," the young man said.

"It could be very dangerous for her," his father worried.

"Not under these circumstances," Claude said.

David Leopold turned to her. "What do you think?"

"I wanted your opinion."

"That places me in a very difficult position," he said.

"I'm sorry."

Claude said, "You needn't give an opinion if you'd rather not."

The old man sighed. "In that case I'd rather not." He told her. "I think you should do what your own instinct dictates. I very much doubt if that young ski instructor is the villain Claude chooses to think him. But there is, of course, always a doubt."

"Thank you," she said. "You have given me an opinion of sorts."

They left the old man alone in the study again and went out to the reception hall. She told Claude, "I'd better get dressed for meeting Rolf."

He said, "Then you're going to do as I suggested?"

"Yes. You so obviously want me to."

"It will be all right," he said seriously.

"I hope so," she said.

She went upstairs in a confused state of mind. She didn't look forward to the evening ahead with Rolf Monner. But she knew how obstinate Claude was when he had an idea in his head and she hoped to clear this part of the mystery up. When she returned from the evening out she hoped that she'd be able to assure Claude that Rolf was completely innocent. Ever since the afternoon she'd talked with Otto Fess she'd had strong feelings that he might be the phantom. He was a strange old man, obsessed with loyalty to the Nazi tradition, and perhaps mad.

She put on a smart ski pants outfit and knitted cap and went down to wait for Rolf. On the way down she met Gretchen coming up the stairs. The blonde girl took in her outfit with a look of mock amazement.

"You prefer night skiing?" she asked.

Ina blushed. "I'm going out for a drive and I want to be warm and comfortable. This is the best outfit for it I have."

Gretchen gave her a jeering look. "I know who you're going driving with," she said.

"Do you?"

"Rolf," she said. "Father told me. He's very upset about it."

Ina felt angry. It was impossible to have any secrets in the old castle. She said, "He had no right to tell you."

"I don't care," Gretchen said airily. "Rolf and I finished with each other ages ago." And she went on by Ina.

She went on downstairs feeling more than a little annoyed. Claude was there waiting for her and he eyed her with a look of approval.

"I must say you're very pretty tonight," he told her.

"Thank you," she said. "It's very generous of you sending me out with another man!"

He took her in his arms. "For a purpose!"

"So you say!"

"And I mean it," he told her. "This may break the mystery of Mother's disappearance if you handle him right."

"You think so?"

"I'm certain of it. Plague him with questions. The right questions." And he kissed her.

A few minutes later Rolf was at the door to get her. When he saw Claude standing in the foyer a cloud came across the tall young German's craggy face. He gave Claude a cold nod of greeting and asked her if she were ready. She said she was and they left.

Rolf had his tiny German car and when they were in it he asked her, "What did that mean?"

"What? she asked innocently.

"Claude seeing you off on your date with me. Isn't he jealous?"

"No. I've made it clear to him I'm not interested in musicians."

Rolf lost some of his tension. He even managed a smile. "You prefer the athletic type?"

She smiled. "Tall, muscular and irresistible. Just like you!"

He chuckled as he started the little car. "You are, as they say, joshing me. But I like it. From you I will accept any kind of joke."

They drove along the snowy road and she saw it was another clear, cold night with a spectacular display of stars overhead. She tried to forget that the man behind the wheel could be a dangerous killer. She was helped in this by the fact that she had really never believed it. It was Claude who had put this tag on him. She now noticed they were heading toward the village.

"Where are you taking me?" she asked.

"I remember you like good beer," he smiled at her. "There is a place I want to show you."

"Your memory is good. You keep the facts about your girls straight!"

Rolf nodded. "Where girls are concerned I have the mind of a computer."

They reached a small tavern with a number of cars parked in front of it and light emanating from its leaded glass windows. You could hear the sound of an accordion playing merrily inside and the murmur of voices. As they left their car Rolf gave her another of his engaging smiles.

"You will like this place," he promised her.

They went inside to a room bursting with people. The tavern keeper had a handle-bar mustache and greeted Rolf and her warmly. But he shrugged and said, "There is only the bar!"

"That will do," Rolf told him. "We're only staying a short time."

They edged their way through the laughing groups from the ski resorts and found a tiny space at the bar. Rolf ordered for them and she watched the beer drawn from the spigot of a huge keg behind the bar. The barman passed them the filled, foaming steins with a smile. She tried the beer and found it bitingly excellent.

"Wonderful!" she said.

"I knew you'd approve," Rolf told her. "I am the perfect escort."

She looked up at the tall young German. "And you are also modest!" she mocked him.

He joined in the fun. "It is my failing!"

She was finishing her beer when she happened to glance down at the shadowed end of the bar and saw that someone was standing there watching her with grim interest. It was the young Englishman whom Gretchen was seeing and it made her at once feel panicky. She began to wonder if they had been followed and what the Englishman and Gretchen might be up to.

She turned to Rolf. "What next?"

"No more beer?" His steely eyes questioned her and she was at once reminded of Claude's theory.

"I've enjoyed it but I've had enough," she said.

"Then we shall move on," Rolf said. He paid the bartender and they pushed their way through the crowd to the door again.

Outside, she said, "The fresh air is so good!"

Rolf gave her a strange piercing glance. "I'm glad you think so, since I'm going to take you to a favorite place of mine."

She had no idea what he meant. Nor did she later when they drove to the bottom of the ski slope and he parked the car there. Then he took her up on the ski-lift to level after level until they had reached the platform of the lodge at the very top of the peak. The lodge was closed now and the ski-lifts were deserted. They had the whole area to themselves. It was as quiet as death and as cold as the grave.

She shuddered as they stood together on the platform. "It's a unique experience but so cold."

"My favorite place," he said, gazing up at the star-studded sky. "Have the heavens ever seemed closer to you?"

"No," she agreed gazing up at them. "You are right."

"Come over by the slopes. It is very pretty by moonlight," he said, leading her away from the platform.

They walked for about five minutes and then stood above the slopes. He said, "I often come here at night and ski alone."

She felt a warning chill seep through her and she looked at him with frightened eyes. "You ski the slopes alone at night?"

"Yes. Why not?"

She gave a tiny, nervous laugh. "People will confuse you with the phantom."

"I think not," he said dryly. And he turned to her. "What do you feel about me, Ina? Could you marry me and live here."

"I've never given it serious thought," she said.

His eyes met hers. "Please do. I want to marry you. I've played around with many women. I think you are the first one I've ever loved."

"And you've told that to them all," she said, studying him as he stood there tall against the snow and the moonlit evergreens.

"This time I am sincere," he assured her.

"Let me think about it," she said evasively, working for time. "I need to know more about you. About your family and how you lived before you came here."

"I lived from hand to mouth," he said. "My father was blinded in the war. I think I told you."

"What was your father's name?" she asked.

"Monner."

"What other name?"

"None that matters," he said. "Let us go back to the lodge. I have keys. We can enjoy a drink and make a log fire and sit before it and talk."

They walked back to the platform and she looked down from its dizzying height. She said, "It's very high. You'd think it would be dangerous. Has anyone ever fallen off?"

Rolf smiled at her. "No. The ones who come up this far are experts and agile. Few reach this point."

It was the last thing he said to her. For at that moment a figure emerged from the shadows behind them and struck him on the back of the head with a bottle. Rolf collapsed with a groan as the phantom in the stocking mask turned his attention to Ina.

When she recovered enough she let out a stunned cry and backed away from the figure of the masked skier. And she was also aware of another masked figure in ski outfit in the background. The second figure stood over the prostrate Rolf as the other one advanced on her.

"No!" she screamed as he came nearer and nearer working her to the very edge of the platform, until she was inches from toppling over to her certain death on the rocks far below.

The masked figure poised as if to shove her over when a shot rang out in the cold night. And for just a second the phantom halted and stood still and then he fell to the ground in a crumpled heap. There was an oath in German from the second masked figure and he came running toward her to finish the job the first one had begun.

But he didn't even get to her before a second shot rang out and he also fell to the platform with his blood reaching out to stain the surrounding snow. Sobbing, she stared down at the two fallen men and edged away from the brink of the platform. As she did so, three other figures emerged from behind the lodge.

She recognized the first as David Leopold. The others were police. The old man came quickly to her and put an arm around her. "Are you all right?"

"Yes," she sobbed. "Who?"

The police had bent down by the first of her assailants, the one she would always think of as the Phantom of the Slopes, and ripped the stocking mask from his face. It was the dead, calm face of Claude Leopold she saw in the moonlight.

"It can't be!" she protested.

"I'm afraid it is," David Leopold said.

"Your son!"

"Not my son," the old man said sadly. "Karl Bruck's son!"

The second masked man stirred and groaned as the police unmasked him. It was the gaunt-faced Otto Fess. Ina turned away from the bloody scene to hurry to Rolf's side. He was already half-sitting up. But still dazed. He stared at her and then at the bodies and the police.

"What is going on here?" he wanted to know.

The elderly David Leopold came to his side. "Plenty of time for that later. Just now we'll look after that wound on your head and get back to the castle."

It was before a blazing fireplace in the drawing room of the castle that David Leopold sat with a grave look on his lined face and told them the whole story.

"Marta played a trick on me in the beginning. She knew

that Karl Bruck had an illegitimate son by a Jewess and that the child had gone to the concentration camps without his father intervening. Through Otto Fess she traced the youngster and then adopted him without telling me who he really was. You can see why she cherished so much love on him."

Ina asked, "But why did he turn against her?"

"He learned that she was planning to write her memoirs and tell the truth about his heritage as a shocker. It was her career against his. He felt he would be ruined if people knew he was the son of the notorious Karl Bruck. So he decided to stop the book being written or published at all costs. He first killed that young German writer and hid his body in the cellars of the castle. And when Marta became suspicious he killed her and destroyed the part of the manuscript concerning him. But he knew you had already been invited to work on the book so he had to deal with you."

"And all the while you were beginning to suspect him?" Rolf said.

"Yes," David Leopold replied. "Only yesterday did I find Marta's decomposed body in the cellar here. I felt it had to be Claude and I told the police so. Then when he suggested you go out with Rolf I knew he had some scheme in mind to kill you and make Rolf seem guilty. I also felt Otto Fess was his accomplice and Gretchen had no part in it."

"So you followed him?" she said.

"Yes. As soon as he left the castle I alerted the police and followed him. He trailed you to the tavern and up the ski-lift. And we followed by another lift and were there when we were needed."

She stared into the flames and said, "And now Claude is dead and Otto Fess is seriously wounded."

"He won't live," David Leopold said. "The police told me that. Just as well. It will be easier for Pauline. She'll never really be aware of what happened. She's so lost in her memories now."

Ina gave the old man a frightened look. "Claude spoke of Rolf's eyes. He claimed that he had Bruck's hypnotic eyes. But now that I recall things clearly I'm sure it was Claude who had his father's strange eyes."

David Leopold rose. "It's all over now. Most of them are dead or dying. Soon the world will forget about them except for the history professors. Will you write Marta's book?

She shook her head. "No. Let it die too," she said.

David Leopold left them alone in the big room before the blazing fire. Rolf's head was bandaged but he looked extremely healthy in spite of this. Awkwardly he turned to her and said, "When all this is over, do you think you could ever bring yourself to marry a German?"

She managed a faint smile. "Perhaps. But he would have to be a very charming German."

With just a hint of his old brashness, he said, "I'm your man! And I promise you I will forget all the others!" And he sealed his promise by taking her in his arms.

GREAT GOTHICS
by
Marilyn Ross

Join the millions who have thrilled to the haunting tales of one of the queens of romantic fiction.
These titles are available now from
Warner Paperback Library.

95¢ each, wherever paperbacks are sold

— **THE DEVIL'S DAUGHTER** (75-002)
— **NIGHT OF THE PHANTOM** (65-960)
— **THE SINISTER GARDEN** (65-935)
— **MISTRESS OF MOORWOOD MANOR** (65-916)
— **THE WITCH OF BRALHAVEN** (65-894)
— **THE LONG NIGHT OF FEAR** (65-864)
— **PHANTOM OF THE SWAMP** (65-829)
— **DARK STARS OVER SEACREST** (65-788)

If you are unable to obtain these books from your local dealer, they may be ordered directly from the publisher. Please allow 4 weeks for delivery. (W)

WARNER PAPERBACK LIBRARY
P.O. Box 3
Farmingdale, New York 11735

Please send me the books I have checked.
I am enclosing payment plus 10¢ per copy to cover postage and handling.

Name ....
Address ....
City .... State .... Zip ....
_____ Please send me your free mail order catalog

FOR SUPERIOR, SPELLBINDING SUSPENSE READ THE MASTERFUL GOTHIC NOVELS OF

Dorothy Daniels

Some Of The Many Fine Dorothy Daniels Novels
Now Available
From WARNER PAPERBACK LIBRARY

___ **THE LARRABEE HEIRESS** (65-981/95¢)
___ **DARK ISLAND** (65-626/95¢)
___ **DIABLO MANOR** (64-650/75¢)
___ **THE BELL** (65-605/95¢)
___ **MAYA TEMPLE** (65-917/95¢)
___ **THE LANIER RIDDLE** (65-909/95¢)
___ **SHADOWS FROM THE PAST** (65-877/95¢)
___ **THE HOUSE ON CIRCUS HILL** (65-844/95¢)
___ **CASTLE MORVANT** (65-816/95¢)
___ **THE HOUSE OF BROKEN DOLLS** (65-778/95¢)
___ **CONOVER'S FOLLY** (65-764/95¢)

If you are unable to obtain these books from your local dealer, they may be ordered directly from the publisher. Please allow 4 weeks for delivery.

WARNER PAPERBACK LIBRARY
P.O. Box 3
Farmingdale, New York 11735
Please send me the books I have checked.
I am enclosing payment plus 10¢ per copy to cover postage and handling.

Name ....
Address ....
City .... State .... Zip ....
_____ Please send me your free mail order catalog

WALK WITH KINGS AND QUEENS

Relive the gilded days of Tudor England....

Visit the lavish court of Henry VIII....

Meet his wives, children, ministers and enemies....

I AM MARY TUDOR by Hilda Lewis

"Bloody Mary" Tudor, daughter of Henry VIII, tells of her role in one of the most fascinating epochs of history.
78-017/$1.50

THE PRIVATE LIFE OF HENRY VIII
by N. Brysson Morrison

Come behind the scenes at Windsor. Listen in on the court intrigues of one of the world's most awesome monarchs.
66-814/$1.25

A CROWN FOR ELIZABETH by Mary M. Luke

The story of Queen Elizabeth I. Her triumphs and her tragedy, told with authority and style.   68-787/$1.50

CATHERINE THE QUEEN by Mary M. Luke

She was Henry VIII's first wife and mother of "Bloody Mary." She won the love of the English people, even as she lost that of her king.   68-743/$1.50

THE PRIVATE LIFE OF HENRY VIII, CATHERINE THE QUEEN and **A CROWN FOR ELIZABETH** are all available in a royally designed slipcase for library permanence.   11-013/$4.25